TO HOPE

A Broken Roads Romance

TO HOPE

•

Carolyn Brown

AVALON BOOKS
NEW YORK

Bro

Published by Thomas Bouregy & Co., Inc.
160 Madison Avenue, New York, NY 10016

Library of Congress Cataloging-in-Publication Data

Brown, Carolyn, 1948-
    To hope / Carolyn Brown.
        p. cm.
    ISBN 978-0-8034-9964-5
    1. Cowgirls—Fiction.   2. Cowboys—Fiction.
3. Rodeos—Fiction.   I. Title.

    PS3552.R685275T585 2009
    813'.54—dc22

                                2009003700

PRINTED IN THE UNITED STATES OF AMERICA
ON ACID-FREE PAPER
BY HADDON CRAFTSMEN, BLOOMSBURG, PENNSYLVANIA

In memory of Charles Earl and
Mary Belle Goshorn—"Grammy and Pappy"

Chapter One

Jodie Cahill woke up cranky. What on Earth had she been thinking when she agreed to go on a three month rodeo circuit with a strange man named James Moses Crowe? She'd given her word and in her world that was as good as gold, but she sure wished she could take it back when it came down to the wire that morning.

What, or rather who, she found sitting in her living room didn't help matters one iota. She had decided to wallow in her grumpy mood no matter where she was or whom she spent the time with. They all four sat there grinning like Cheshire cats who'd just found a bucket of mice floating in pure cream. How could she keep up her self-imposed grumpy mood when those four had come to see her off?

"What in the devil are you doing here?" she asked the four women sipping coffee at six A.M. on a cold, blustery January morning.

"We've come to send you off in style," her sister, Roseanna, said.

Greta, Roseanna's new sister-in-law, yawned. "You think we'd let some old man haul your grouchy heinie out of here without checking him out first?"

Jodie pointed to the door. "Go home."

Dee, a short brunet, shook her head. "Not on your life, darlin'. I didn't get up at the unholy hour of five-thirty and hurry over here just to be sent home. I'm not sure you can go to heaven if you get up this early. It might be one of the deadly sins, and here I am committing it just to cheer you on. Besides, Jack is watching Jaxson and I'm going to enjoy every sip of this coffee and have a second cup."

"Face it," Stella said. "It's what happens when the last one of five doesn't have a husband. They have to put up with the other newlyweds running their lives."

"I do not want a husband and I'm in a mood," Jodie warned them.

At nearly six feet tall and a bull rider to boot, that should have put a little fear into them. It didn't. They kept talking and drinking coffee.

"Warm cinnamon rolls, anyone?" Jodie's mother, Joanna, asked.

Roseanna motioned for her to bring them to the living room. "Long as we can have them in here. We're going to see this man who's carrying Jodie off for three months. We're not sitting in the kitchen and missing a peek at him. I heard he can walk on water."

"Moses, not Jesus," Dee said. "He can part the waters and walk on dry land. You must have been sleeping in Sunday school the day they talked about Moses."

"Must've been," Rosy said. "Anyway he's a man of God who's coming to see if he can straighten up Jodie's halo. Her halo and wings both have been in so many wrecks she's having to buy high-risk insurance on it these days," she teased.

"Oh, the bunch of you can hush," Jodie grinned. She pulled her long, dark brown hair back into a clip at the nape of her neck, tucked her chambray shirt into a pair of tight-fitting jeans, and buckled her belt—all with one hand. If she could ride a bull with one hand in the air, she could dang well take care of herself with one hand. Some of the mundane daily chores now took twice as long as usual but she hadn't asked for help yet, and didn't plan to start.

"She smiled," Stella announced. "We at least got her out of that mood before he gets here."

"I'm warning you all. He's a short, stocky, barrel-chested, nearly bald Native American with a big, round face and a belly that hangs over his belt like an inner tube. What do you expect with a name like James Moses Crowe? You're all going to be disappointed when I'm right," Jodie said.

Her suitcase, garment and boot bags, and a paper sack with snacks for the first day in the pickup truck waited beside the door. She hoped James hated cheese crackers and pretzels and that he wasn't prone to long-winded conversations about his six kids and forty-eight pets.

Four days ago she was all excited about getting back into the rodeo and bull-riding circuit, and then she fell on a patch of ice and broke her left wrist. She'd barely gotten home from the emergency room when the phone call came from the Professional Bull Rider's CEO to finalize plans. She'd had to tell him the news. At least she'd had the foresight to get a doctor's release. Rules said without the release she would have paid fines for skipping each of the twenty events she'd already entered. The rules also stated that she'd have to add another ten days before she would be eligible to compete in any PBR competition after the cast was removed. With that much time lost, there was no way she could come out with enough points to compete in the Built Ford Tough Series competition in the fall. It was a heart breaker but she'd live through it.

The next day the CEO called with an offer. She refused at first and should have kept right on turning it down. But she'd been angry at the turn of events and figured she might as well be in the excitement, even if she couldn't ride. At least it looked that way three days ago. Now she wasn't so sure. She'd agreed to judge events in eighteen cities in the next three months, and James Moses Crowe was the man she'd be keeping company with all those weeks and miles.

Roseanna heard the vehicle and hurried over to peek out the front window. "Jodie, you are dead wrong."

Dee joined her. "*Whew*! That's not baldheaded, and he's not old enough to have six kids. Honey, I don't know jack squat about rodeos or bull riding, but I'll trade places with you."

"Oh, both of you hush," Jodie said. "You're just saying that to make me look and then you'll laugh at me."

Stella joined them. "Joanna, he's here and you might want to give this man his walking orders before you let your daughter go off with him. He's liable to steal her heart."

"I'm twenty-six years old," Jodie moaned. "Y'all are acting like second-graders. Get out of the way and let me see. Good God Almighty!"

Greta sighed. "Yes, ma'am. There sits thirty thousand dollars worth of car. I'd love to get that thing out on the road and open it up full blast. I betcha that's the original paint job too. They don't make that shade of dynasty green anymore, and I'll also betcha it's got a two-tone pony interior. Pretty ain't it?"

"Maybe in your world. In the world of rodeo, he's a dead man," Jodie said.

Jimmy Crowe parked a vintage 1965 Ford Mustang in the front yard of the house and sat for a moment, staring at the place. It hadn't changed much in twenty-one years. There was still a big lodge over to the left after he made the turn onto the Cahill property. Trees lined the lane to the ranch house a quarter of a mile on down the road just like they did all those years ago. The house had been painted white. He remembered it pale yellow and it didn't look nearly as big as it did when he was a little boy.

Nothing had changed, but he had. Jimmy wasn't a shy kindergartener anymore. He was an established free-lance writer and photographer. After this trip, he'd have enough information to fill in the blanks on a mystery novel he'd been working on for two years. He already had a publisher with money in hand, ready to buy the book. Yes, Jimmy had changed. He wondered if Jodie Cahill was still the same.

Leaving his long black overcoat folded on the top of his suitcases and laptop in the back seat; he opened the door and stretched his legs, kicking his pants legs down over his shoes. He stood just over six feet tall, had blond hair that lay in curls on his shirt collar, and eyes almost the same shade as his car. He wore a dark green silk shirt tucked into pleated black dress slacks.

*   *   *

Jodie moaned again as she watched him make his way to the door. "He's got tassels on his shoes. Lord, what have I gotten myself into?"

Greta almost swooned. "If I wasn't so much in love with Kyle, I'd trade you."

"You can have both of them," Jodie said just before she swung open the front door. "Come in, Mr. Crowe. I'm packed and ready, and we've got a long way to go. I thought we were taking your vehicle, but I see I was wrong."

"Hello, Jodie. We *are* taking my car," he said.

There wasn't a bit of recognition in her face. That was good. She had absolutely no idea. She'd been a tall child, and now she was a tall woman. He could've picked her out of a lineup, though. The eyes were still the same shade of aqua—not blue, not green. The braids had been replaced with a stylish cut she had pulled back into a pony tail with a clip. Jeans cinched a small waist. Jodie, all grown up, was enough to take his breath away, but he'd get over it in the next three months. Or else he'd have to buy his best friend and therapist a steak dinner.

Roseanna cleared her throat.

"Excuse me, Mr. Crowe, this is my sister, Rosy." Jodie tried to make nice.

Rosy shook hands with him. "It's a pleasure to meet you. How did you know which one of us was Jodie?"

Jimmy thought fast. "Cast on her arm. That's why she's going with me and not Sawyer Carver, remember?"

Jodie was getting grumpier by the moment. "This is Rosy's sister-in-law, Greta."

"That is one sweet car. Is it a family heirloom or . . ."

Jimmy shook hands again. "No, I just like vintage cars. It's nice to meet you, Greta."

"Got a two-eighty-nine and auto on the console?" Greta almost salivated.

"You know your cars," he said.

"She should. She drives too fast and has wrecked enough of them," Rosy said.

"A woman after my own heart," Jimmy smiled.

"And I'm Stella, and this is Dee. We're just friends who came to see Jodie off to the rodeos." She stuck out her hand.

"It's a pleasure to meet you all. Are you ready?" he asked Jodie.

"James, I am Joanna, Jodie's mother. Would you care for cinnamon rolls and coffee before y'all leave?"

"I've had breakfast but thank you very much. They smell wonderful," he said. The rolls did smell heavenly, but he was too nervous to eat. Dee, Stella, or Jodie's mother could recognize him any minute.

Jodie leaned against the front door. "I am ready but we are definitely not going in that car out there."

"Why?"

"Why did you pull strings with the association and get them to talk me into going with you? Answer me that?"

"Because your insight into the rodeo world will be

invaluable to me in my coverage for the newspaper and the magazines I'm working with as well as the novel I'm writing. Got to admit, I'm not much of a Western man," he said.

"So you want to see what it's really like to travel all those miles and miles on the road instead of flying from one event to the other?"

"That's right," he said.

"Then we're going in my pickup truck. There's not a cowboy out there who'd be riding in a vintage automobile. If I'm going, we're taking my truck," she said.

Stubborn as a cross-eyed mule, he thought. She hadn't changed one bit in that respect. She'd set her heels and it didn't look like a team of wild steers could budge her.

"Oh, get over it, Jodie," Greta said. "What difference does it make what you ride in or he drives? Either way gets you from point A to B."

"He wants to write about rodeos and bull riding, he's going to do it in a truck. Or maybe you can't drive a stick shift? Is that the problem?" she taunted.

His green eyes narrowed into slits. "I can drive anything with wheels. We'll take your truck, Jodie. It'll save a lot of mileage on my car anyway. Do you at least have a garage where I can park it?"

"Yes, you can put it where my truck is parked, and we'll even shut the garage door so Greta won't drool on it." Jodie led the way from the living room, through the kitchen, and out the back door into the garage. She pushed a button and the doors went up. She tossed him a set of keys she picked from a hook beside the door. "Back it out and put your car in its place. You get half the back seat for your things. I'll bring my things out the front door."

"I'll get your bags. You have a broken arm," Jimmy said between clenched teeth.

"I have one broken arm. Not two," she said.

"Have it your way."

"Don't take that tone with me."

"Then don't be so high and mighty."

In the background she heard Roseanna giggling. It wasn't funny, dang it all anyway. She wasn't about to show up at a rodeo in that car, beautiful as it was. He'd blame her and whine like a girl when someone damaged the paint job. Besides, if he really wanted to see the way rodeo people lived, then he could start right now.

Jodie threw her leather bomber jacket in the back seat. Not one of those hussies she called family and friends offered to help her load her things. It had taken three trips but she'd managed without them.

Jimmy unloaded a trunkload of stuff, filling his half of the backseat to the brim. She noted a laptop, two suitcases, a bulging garment bag, and two briefcases. He locked his car, patted it on the hood, and crawled into the pickup.

"You said this was a stick shift," he said.

"No, I asked if you could drive a stick shift," she answered tersely.

"Give me the keys. I can see this is going to be a long three months."

She handed them to him. "You know how to get to Dallas from here?"

"You'll tell me, I'm very sure," he said.

"Yes, I will. Take a left at the park entrance and go over to Davis. We'll catch Interstate 35 there and go south to Dallas where we'll get Interstate 20 to Mobile, Alabama. From there it's a little more than three hundred miles to Pensacola where we catch Interstate 75 South. I can take you to the St. Lucie County Fairgrounds in Fort Pierce, Florida, with my eyes shut. Why are you here, Mr. Crowe?"

"I've already answered that. I'm here to write freelance stories and get first-hand experience so I can finish a book I'm working on. Brad told him he'd informed you of my intentions and I told you the same thing back at the house. And your job is to ride with me and give me the inside information on bull riders. In trade you get all expenses paid plus payment each time you judge an event. Did I pass that test? And the name is Jimmy, not Mr. Crowe. I'm willing to bet we are close to the same age."

"Twenty-six on my last birthday, which was in August," she said. She smelled a rat in the wood pile. Something wasn't totally right and yet nothing seemed wrong.

"Twenty-six on my last birthday, which was in May," he said.

She nodded and checked the speedometer: a comfortable five miles over the speed limit. A policeman might point at him but most likely wouldn't pull him over for a ticket.

"Sawyer was disappointed when you broke your wrist. He's followed your career ever since you climbed on your first bull. But then you probably knew that," Jimmy said.

"No, I didn't. Momma keeps all the news and magazine articles in a collection of scrapbooks. I don't remember his name on any of them."

"Sawyer's pen name is Thomas Klinger. Does that ring a bell?"

She sat straight up. "*The* Thomas Klinger. The famous sports writer? Every time he mentioned me in an article I walked on air for days. That's Sawyer Carver! And I missed getting to go on the rounds with him because I broke my arm and can't ride. Now I really am cranky."

"Sorry I mentioned it then if it'll make you worse. I'm sure he is too, if it's any consolation. His wife told me that he was in a royal pout. He refused to do the rodeo rounds and is opting to go to Peru for a month to follow soccer finals. I'll be covering for him as well as freelancing for a couple of magazines while we are out."

"He's married?" She frowned.

"Thirty-five years and lives in New York with his wife and two poodles. They have two daughters but they're both married and have children of their own."

"Are you married?"

"No, ma'am," he said in a soft Texas drawl. "Never have been. How about you?"

She shook her head. So he was twenty-six; too pretty with those dimples that really weren't dimples but long wrinkles that creased his angular cheeks when he smiled. And he wasn't married. She chanced a long look at him. No, not her type. She liked them rugged, with dark hair and arms big enough to heft a steer.

"What kind of music do you like?"

"Country," she said quickly. *Please, God, don't let him like classical or, worse yet, rap.*

With his right hand he reached into the back seat of the club cab truck and brought out a zippered folder. "Pick your poison."

"CDs? But an old Mustang wouldn't have a CD player. Why did you bring these?"

"I had it customized. I expect you have a player in this thing?"

She pushed a button and a slim drawer slid out. He didn't tell her that he already knew she was a country music fan or that the folder was filled with her favorite music.

"So you like country music too?"

"My favorite."

Jodie leaned back on the seat, shut her eyes, and listened to Kenny Chesney sing about how forever feels. The ice was broken, and it didn't look like it was going to be such a bad trip after all. Jimmy liked country music. At least she had that to offset tassels on his shoes.

At noon she turned off the music and began looking at the signs. "I'm hungry."

"Fast food for lunch and a good dinner or the opposite?"

"I don't care if it's bologna sandwiches for both. I get grouchy when I'm hungry. If you aren't going to find a place to eat pretty soon, I'll drag out my crackers."

"You are easy."

"Is that a compliment or a derogatory remark?"

He smiled and the dimples deepened. "Take it however you want to. Next exit has McDonalds, Subway, pizza, or Hardees."

"McDonalds."

He nodded and put on the blinker. So she was cranky when he picked her up that morning. She didn't mind fast food and got grouchy when she was hungry. He wondered what made her happy.

"I'll be with you in a minute. Check the menu and have your order ready," he said as he headed toward the men's room.

She didn't need to check the menu. She knew what she liked at McDonalds, Burger King, Taco Bell, and most of the other fast food places along the way. She sat down at a booth where she could read the menu board just in case she did change her mind and decided to try one of their new sandwiches. She hadn't talked herself into anything different by the time he joined her.

"Ready?"

She nodded.

"I'll have a double quarter pounder with cheese, large fries, and a large drink," she told the cashier.

"The chipotle wrap, a fruit parfait, and a medium drink." He ordered and handed the woman a Visa card.

She stared at his meager lunch. "What did you eat for breakfast?"

"I had a bran muffin and a fruit smoothie. Why do you ask?"

She bit into the burger. "You're twenty-six, not eighty-six. Why would you eat old people food?"

He waved toward her pile of french fries loaded with salt and pepper. "You are clogging your arteries with all that fat."

"No, I'm not. I work hard so I can eat good. It's people like you that sit on your hind ends all day in an office that have to eat like you are already looking St. Peter in the eyeball."

"You are eating almost fifteen hundred calories and more than seventy fat grams in that meal right there. And I'd guess you are drinking soda with sugar, not diet?"

"You got it, honey. And I'm having a hot caramel sundae after I finish so don't put that Visa card away too deeply. You can add the calories and fat grams from that too."

He shuddered.

She giggled.

So that's what made her happy. Fat-filled food that would give her a heart attack before she was fifty. He wasn't surprised, not when he thought about her at five years old. No one picked on Jodie Cahill, and it wasn't because Roseanna took up for her either. It was because Jodie didn't take a bit of guff from anyone, boys or girls. With that attitude she probably had her veins and fat cells beaten into submission. They were afraid to hang onto an extra bit of cholesterol.

"Were you a fat little boy who got teased and pushed around or something? Bet that's it. You were chubby and when you were a teenager you went on one of those diets that only let you eat water and celery sticks. Now you've got this obsession with fat grams and calories and preach it at every meal." She dipped fries in ketchup and talked between bites.

"I've never been fat," he said flatly.

"Hey, I didn't mean to offend you. I've always been a big eater. I work it off most days. By the end of this trip, I might gain five pounds but it'll all come off when I get home because spring will put me in the fields from daylight to dark."

"You like ranching?"

"Love it. Can't imagine anything else. My sisters all

went to college, and Momma and Daddy were determined I'd follow in their footsteps. I tried one semester. Couldn't stand it. Went home and told Daddy I'd rather shovel manure. I've been ridin' the rodeo rounds or ranching ever since. Got a herd of cattle and a couple of horses that are mine. Help with the ranch and when Granny Etta needs it, she runs a bed and breakfast called Cahill Lodge. You might've noticed it when you turned down our lane. Anyway, I help her out some too. Mostly nowadays Granny is out galavantin' around with her best friend, Roxie Hooper, and Rosy runs the lodge so I help her now that Greta isn't there anymore. But that's another story." She was rambling.

"No offense taken, then," he said curtly and finished the yogurt parfait.

She polished off the last bits of fries. "You going to get my sundae or is dessert not on the expense account?"

"Are you serious?"

"As the heart attack you think it will cause," she said.

"I'll get it," he said. "Hot caramel, right? One or two?"

She smiled. Even with a tiny fleck of ketchup still hanging on the corner of her mouth she was sexy as hell. The one thing she didn't look like was a bull rider. A model perhaps with those long legs and height. A movie star with that delicate nose and full mouth. Definitely not a woman who crawled on the back of a bull named Demon or White Lightning and held on for eight seconds.

"One will do until snack time in the middle of the afternoon. And get a large coffee to go," she smarted right back at him.

Familiar landmarks went by at seventy-five miles an hour. She'd been down this same road many times, at first with her father driving and alone after high school graduation. It was the first time she'd traveled it with a total stranger. Even if she knew his birth month, that he hadn't been a chubby kid, and that he was a friend of Thomas Klinger, he was still a stranger. With that icy aura surrounding him, she figured he probably would remain a stranger the day they finished the circuit and he took her back to Sulphur, Oklahoma.

Sometime in the late afternoon, about the time he was watching carefully for Exit 73, which would put them on US 49 South toward Richland/Hattiesburg, his cell phone began to ring. He was driving behind a semi with no place to go and couldn't see the road signs until they were already gone.

He picked up the ringing phone from the console and pitched it in her lap. "Here, answer this and tell whoever it is that I'll call them back."

"Aye, aye, sir!" She flipped the phone open and said, "Hello."

"Who is this?" A deep voice asked.

"This is Jodie. I'm supposed to tell whoever is calling that Jimmy will call you back. Name and number please? Of course, the answering machine could have told him that if he hadn't been so rattled about a semi blocking all the signs, and I wouldn't have to be talking to you, whoever you are."

The voice chuckled. "So the infamous Jodie answers the phone. Tell him to call his therapist when he has time. I'll be out after six tonight but it's important that I speak to him so please tell him to call before six."

"And why do you think I'm infamous? Are you a rodeo fan?"

"Let's just say I've heard of you and leave it at that. Will you please tell Jimmy to call me?"

"Will do," she said.

Tassels on his shoes. Watches his diet. A therapist. God Almighty, does one of those bags back there contain Prozac by the bucketful too? I'm traveling with a neurotic who can't survive without daily visits from his therapist. And I thought Rosy's husband, Trey, was a prissy city boy.

Jimmy successfully caught the off ramp. "Who was it?"

"Your therapist. He said to call him before six and it was important."

"That would be Paul. I suppose we'll be in our hotel by six so that won't be a problem. Now, how many miles do we stay on this highway?"

He doesn't even blush? He has a therapist at the age of twenty-six and he doesn't even deny it or turn red?

"Little more than eighty miles, then we'll catch

Interstate 59 South for about ten miles. Then it's about ninety miles to Mobile. That's the halfway mark, or do you want to drive farther today and less tomorrow? I don't have to be at the riding until tomorrow night, so we can make Fort Pierce easy by then if we leave early. We'll be there two nights, and then do some heavy driving to make it to Denver by the night of the eighth."

"Mobile is fine. That will give me plenty of time to get in touch with Paul."

"So why do you see a therapist?"

"You don't?" he asked.

"No, I do not! I'm well-adjusted. Only prone to be cranky or grouchy when I have to give up something I really want. Like this riding circuit. I don't need a therapist. Why do you?"

He blushed. Deep crimson filled his cheeks. "It's personal."

She waited.

"Paul isn't a real therapist. He's my best friend, and I tell him everything so he teases and says he's my therapist."

Lord, it just got deeper and deeper.

"That sounds kind of sissy," she said.

"Men can have best friends. Do you ever watch the television series 'House'?"

"Love it. Hugh Laurie's character is after my own dear heart."

"What about Wilson? The oncologist on the show?"

She wondered where this was going, and why he'd changed the subject. "What about him?"

"I'm House. Paul is Wilson. We are both writers like they are doctors. We've been friends forever like they have. Does that explain?"

"A little," she said. "So instead of Vicodan you take Prozac? Are you as mean as he is?"

He was visibly appalled. "No, I do not take Prozac and I hope I'm not that mean!"

"If you aren't depressed, what's your problem that's so big you have to visit with Paul daily?"

"Personal and I'm not going there. Change the subject. Talk to me about something else."

"No thanks. I'm taking a nap." She fluffed up the pillow and laid it against the window. She shut her eyes but didn't sleep. She'd make him tell her what his problem was by the end of three months. She wondered what Paul looked like. Did he dress in tight jeans and wear cowboy boots . . . without tassels? Was he rugged, with black hair and dark eyes, or too pretty like Jimmy?

They reached the Econolodge at 5:00. Jimmy booked two rooms with a connecting door and pushed a luggage carrier back out to the parking lot.

She leaned against the fender and waited. "I need that suitcase right there and my sack of snacks."

"What about the rest of it?" he asked.

"That's all I need to take into the hotel," she said.

He piled every scrap of his belongings onto the cart. "Okay."

She followed him into the lobby and down a hallway to an elevator. "You don't travel much, do you?"

"All the time. I seldom get to stay home a whole week. I like to have my own things. It makes traveling easier," he explained.

I'm going to gag if he sets up pictures of his girlfriend, his momma, and pet Chihuahua in the hotel room. My appetite will be ruined by the time I get back home. Even Chris will start lookin' good compared to Jimmy Crowe.

He flipped out a folding suitcase holder in her room and set her luggage on it, put her sack on the dresser, and pushed his mountain of comfort through the connecting door. "We'll find a good restaurant for supper as soon as I unpack and make a few calls. Do you have a preference since you know this part of the country better than I do?"

"There's a wide variety or we can have pizza delivered if we want to stay in and munch on leftovers all evening," she said.

"You decide." He shut the door.

She heard the lock engage and groaned. She heard him talking, most likely to Paul. She envisioned him setting up a china tea set on the table in his room. Even with her ear pressed to the door, she couldn't make out a single word, only a chuckle and his tone.

He doesn't really carry around china, she scolded herself. *Give the man a chance. But he unpacks! He takes all those clothes out of the bags and puts them in drawers for just one night. How can I give a man like that a chance?*

The silent mental argument went on long after she'd opened her suitcase, retrieved a brush, and removed the tangles from her hair. It was still in progress when he knocked on the door and carefully inched it open.

"Have you decided on supper? If you haven't, I think I would like to order pizza. I can get some work done if we don't have to go out," he said.

She turned from the mirror. "Hey, that's fine. I'm a junk food junkie when I travel. What kind do you eat? I'll order."

"Whatever you like," he said.

"Meatlovers?"

"Half black olive and half mushroom. And not a word from you about it either."

"Who me?" She said in wide-eyed innocence.

Without an invitation he sat down at the tiny bistro table in the corner. "Yes, you."

She thumbed through the folder on the dresser, found a pizza place willing to deliver, and made the call. "One large meatlovers and a large with half black olive and half mushrooms with extra cheese."

He groaned.

She hung up. "Live a little. You got plenty of room in your fancy pleated pants to put on a pound or two."

Chapter Two

"**L**adies and gentlemen, how'd you like those opening ceremonies?"

Applause and catcalls filled the arena.

"Welcome to the St. Lucie County Fairgrounds and the Annual Bud Light US Smokeless Tobacco Company Challenger Tour. Tonight you will see the toughest, meanest bulls we could rustle up and the riders who think they're tougher. Please welcome our judges. Fred Massey from Houston, Texas, who retired with more than one championship under his golden buckle. And a newcomer to the judging round but well qualified and not a stranger to the profession. Miss Jodie Cahill from Sulphur, Oklahoma, who won the gold buckle six years ago as the youngest female rider to win it. She's been riding since before she can remember. The judge on the back of the chute tonight is Terrance Roswell. Let's give it up for the judges, the riders, and even the rangy old bulls before the competition begins." The announcer's voice filled the convention center and the ensuing applause was deafening. He gave it time to settle before going on. "If you'll all stand for the National Anthem presented by one of our judges, Jodie Cahill, and remain standing for a moment of silence for our troops."

Jodie picked up the microphone as quiet filled the stands. Clowns placed their hands over their hearts. Cowboys and cowgirls held hats over their hearts. Jimmy stopped taking notes to feel the ambience of the crowd as Jodie stole their hearts with her soulful rendition of the National Anthem. When the last note died and everyone bowed their heads, he knew in that moment this trip was exactly what he needed. He could never have described the feelings without having been there.

The announcer ended the silence with a boom. "Let's ride bulls."

Jimmy picked up his notebook.

Jodie picked up her scorecard.

"First up is Benny Tennyson riding a new bull named Sin. Eighteen hundred pounds of pure mean . . ."

Jodie watched carefully, noting every move the rider made and awarding or deducting points fairly. Eight seconds lasted eight years for the judges as well as the rider, who managed to hang on until the bell sounded.

It was going to be a good season if they all showed that kind of talent. She tallied up her scores and was surprised to see that she and Fred had each awarded forty points. She'd been apprehensive that she'd score too highly. After the first ride, she settled into the job and the evening was over too fast.

Jimmy found her in the middle of riders, both male and female, members of the medical team that followed the PBR rounds and fans when the evening ended. He'd booked them a room for one night at the Radisson Beach Resort on Hutchison Island and had hired a taxi to bring them to the fairgrounds. He'd gotten the phone number and planned to call the same company to take them back to the hotel immediately after the event. His notebook was full and his mind was racing; he wanted to get back to his laptop and put in several hours while it was all fresh.

He touched her elbow. "Are you ready?"

Shivers tap danced down her neck. She attributed it to the first night's excitement of the rounds. "No, I'm going for breakfast with some of the riders. It's tradition. You can go with us. It'll be good for you. If you want personal insight, here it is. IHOP after midnight out at Port St. Lucie. It's where everyone goes."

He couldn't refuse to go but his heart wasn't in it. He wanted to write about the way the dust boiled up under the bull's hooves. The way the clowns drew the big raging monster's attention away from the rider so he could dash to safety. He had a thousand questions to ask Jodie.

She ate pancakes, eggs, bacon, sausage, gravy and hash browns. He watched in amazement that someone so thin could put away so much food. Everyone knew her, and she introduced him to so many people that his mind was in a boggle. He'd never remember all those names or faces, but she'd been right. The camaraderie after the event and good-hearted jesting certainly did add another dimension to the stories he'd send off later that night. And it was invaluable to the detail in the novel he was producing.

It was 2:00 when he called for the taxi and that was amid a bevy of people offering to take them to their hotel, along with a few whistles after she'd told them he'd booked a night at the Radisson and that she intended to spend part of the next day sitting on the beach even if it was cold.

The digital clock rolled up an even 3:00 when he sat down with his laptop and began to record the names of both riders and bulls and the results of the evening. Sunrays streamed through the crack in the draperies by the time he emailed the stories. He yawned and stretched at the same time Jodie knocked on the connecting door.

"Come in!" he yelled.

She threw the door open. She wore soft pink sweat pants and a matching hooded, zip-front jacket over a darker pink tank top. She was still barefoot and her hair hadn't been brushed. He thought she was even more beautiful than she'd been the night before in her tight Western-cut black slacks and matching rhinestone studded jacket.

"Have you had any sleep?"

"Not yet but my stories are done and sent. Have you slept?"

"Four hours. I'm going to the beach to read a book. Want to join me? You can sleep in one of the reclining lawn chairs."

"Sure," he said and wondered if he'd really agreed. There was a king-sized bed not five feet away. Why should he sleep in an uncomfortable chair?

"The sun is bright but there's a nippy breeze. I reckon you'd freeze in those silk pajama bottoms. You got any sweats or . . ."

"I brought a sweat suit to exercise in," he said.

"Then put it on while I find my shoes."

It wasn't the first time Jimmy had pulled an all-nighter writing an article and getting it out to press. It *was* the first time he'd lain outside in the warm sun afterward. The tension eased out of his aching back, and he slept as soundly as if he'd been in his own bed in Austin, Texas.

Jodie opened a big thick romance novel. She had never read the author's writing before but Stella had given her several books to tuck into her baggage for days like this and it was among them. The back of the book said the writer would bring her fans a story with all the promise and passion of forbidden love.

The front of the book had calla lilies on it, at least until she'd opened the cover to find the man of her dreams looking deeply into a red-haired hussy's eyes, his lips only inches from hers, one hand on her hip and the other around her waist. She sighed and opened it to the beginning paragraph; it said that from the first time the gorgeous hunk of man saw the woman he knew she'd never be anyone's bride, or something like that. Jodie looked over at Jimmy, snoring ever so softly. Heavy lashes rested on his high cheekbones. His blond curls falling around his ears and down to his shirt collar reminded her of a little boy she'd seen in television commercials. For someone so into style when it came to his clothing, he looked as if he needed a haircut all the time and never needed to shave.

She sighed. Too bad he couldn't look like the man on the cover of the book. Not exactly Fabio but a good substitute. But then she wasn't a buxom redhead with porcelain skin wearing a blue dress with a ripped bodice. She fell asleep about the time she finished reading about the hero having a well-furnished library. She wondered if Jimmy had a room lined from floor to ceiling with books of his liking. Did he read mystery, westerns, thrillers? Or was he one of those nonfiction readers?

His grumbling stomach awoke him just before noon.

For a moment he couldn't get his bearings. He sat straight up, staring out at endless water and sky of the same color, wondering how he got outside. Then he remembered and yawned. He looked across the space at Jodie, who had an open paperback book over her eyes.

Great God in heaven. There was an ounce of femininity in the lady after all! She read romances. He carefully lifted the book to see what it was about. One of those bodice-rippers he'd seen advertised. He smiled and opened the book. Does she really like this kind of folderol? He would have bet she read true crime or mysteries.

She awoke with a start, sunrays blaring down into her eyes. "Where's my book?"

He handed it back to her. "Right here."

"Guess I dropped it," she said.

"Guess so."

"What time is it?"

He checked his watch. "Eleven thirty."

"Time to get it together and check out," she said.

"This is insane," he grumbled as they trudged through white sand toward the hotel. "We can keep the room another day even if we aren't planning to spend the whole night."

"It's saving money for a later day when we'll want to stay somewhere nice again. No sense in overdoing the expense account. Besides what are you going to do all afternoon? Do you need a place to send anything on the computer?"

"No," he grouched.

"Then we'll check out, have lunch, spend some time in the town and find a McDonald's so I can change in their bathroom for tonight's event," she said.

"And I suppose all the riders do this kind of thing?"

"Hell, no. The riders can't afford to stay in a Radisson on the beachfront. They'll be living in a trailer they're pulling behind their truck or a cheap hotel as close to the fairgrounds as possible. This is a treat, not the norm. I don't expect this kind of expense account, really, I don't. We might even go visiting among the trailers this afternoon so you can see that side of the business. I bet one of the gals will let me change in her trailer. Now that's an idea. Go pack up your things. Think you can get it done in half an hour? I'm hungry. Let's eat at Cracker Barrel. When we leave tonight after the ride, we'll probably only stop for fast food or sandwiches until we reach Denver. You're fixin' to find out the joys of riding for thirty hours, pard'ner."

They had one minute to spare when he handed the room keys to the lady behind the checkout desk. Jodie had already put her suitcase in the truck but his were loaded onto the baggage cart. The lunch rush was almost over by the time they reached the restaurant on I-95. She ordered chicken and dumplings, red beans, fried okra, collard greens, hash brown casserole, and sweet tea.

"And bring biscuits and cornbread before the meal with some honey and blackberry jam," she said.

"Yes, ma'am, and you sir?" the waitress asked.

"I'll have grilled chicken tenders, carrots, and green beans," he said.

Jodie rolled her eyes at him. "You won't make me feel guilty."

"I'm not trying to."

"After I finish this, I'm ordering an apple dumpling for dessert," she said.

"Have at it," he said. The woman was going to break a three-hundred-pound scale if she didn't slow down.

"So tell me about judging. How do you score the riders?"

"You wrote an article about bull riding and you don't even know that?"

"I wrote from the spectator's view. Don't get so up in my face about it, Jodie," he said.

She sipped the tea and buttered a biscuit. "I did, didn't I? I'm sorry. Okay, it goes like this at the PBR events. Three judges are hired. Two judges have 50 points to distribute for each ride. That's 25 points for the bull, and 25 points for the rider. The third judge is the one who's on the back of the bucking chute where the ride starts out. He keeps score in the event that a tie-breaker is needed.

Four judges officiate the PBR Built Ford Tough Series World Finals held in Las Vegas."

"What would make you take off points to the rider or the bull?"

"If the rider touches himself or the bull with his free hand—that's the one up in the air—he's disqualified. Other things he would be docked for would be poor body position or loss of control. We give points for spurring the bull and call them style points. The bull points come from how hard it is to ride the critter. We look for bulls with speed, power, drop in the front end, kick in the back end, and those who can change directions and roll the body. The more of those characteristics he displays, the higher his score, which brings up the total score. Serious riders want a mean bull."

"Did you?"

"The meaner, the better. If he kicked and threw him a little hissy fit out there, it just made more points for me."

"What would scare you?"

"Down in the well. Thinking about that gives me the hives. I had it happen twice. Had some fine bullfighters or I'd be a thing of the past right now. Once it was with Demon Twister. He could've cost me the rest of the rounds."

"What is down in the well?"

"It's a bad situation when a bull spins in one direction and the force of the spin pulls the rider into the motion's vortex. The rider often gets hung up to the bull."

"What do you mean, 'hung up'?"

"It's when the rider isn't able to free his riding hand from his bull rope and is literally hung up to the bull. Thank goodness for bullfighters when that happens. They move in and help get it untangled."

"Did it cost you points?"

"Yep."

"How in the devil did you get back on another one?"

"I got a reride and drew a meaner bull than Demon Twister. Figured it was like falling off a bicycle. If I didn't get on that critter and show him who was boss, I'd never get over the fear."

"You do that with all things that scare you?" he asked.

"Mostly. Face it down or have it control me. I don't like things that control me," she said.

"What does it take to be a professional bull rider?"

"You got to be 18 years of age to purchase a PBR membership. Then you can get your riding permit, which lets you enter the PBR's U.S. Smokeless Tobacco Company Challenger Tour events and the PBR's Enterprise Tour events and the PBR's Discovery Tour events. Once you win $2,500 in prize money, they upgrade your permit status to cardholder status. Then you've got to win that much every year to keep up the cardholder status. I barely made it the last five years. I won the buckle in Las Vegas six years ago when I was just twenty years old. I was all gung ho to do it again the next year but living got in the way. I thought I was ready this year, then this happened." She held up her arm.

"How long have you been riding?"

Their food arrived and she started eating, talking between bites. "I rode my first mutton when I was three. Didn't win a prize but I did the next year after I'd practiced all year. Went to bulls when I was about nine."

"I'll have to ask these questions again when I have my notepad handy," he said.

"Oh, you mean you don't have one of those remember-everything memories?"

"Not quite," he said.

"It's because you don't eat right," she teased. "Your poor little fat cells are empty and starving. It depletes the ability to remember what you've been told. In the future, researchers will find that hungry fat cells are what cause Alzheimer's."

"Then you should have a good memory when you are a hundred and ten years old," he said.

"I plan on giving it my best shot. Here, help me eat this apple dumpling and then we'll go visitin'. All you'll get for supper is what you can find at the fairgrounds so you'd better eat well."

She knocked on trailer doors, and they visited all afternoon. He picked up enough bull-riding lingo to fill pages and pages in his notebook. Everyone was eager to tell their stories and answer questions. Jodie had truly given him entrance into another world, one that would enhance his book for sure, but would also give his press releases a beating heart and breath. Tonight's article would include the human element of trailer life and the bologna sandwiches they shared with one of the up-and-coming female riders, the camaraderie away from the chutes as well as the competition inside the arena among the riders.

He was ready for the opening ceremony that night. An extravaganza within itself, it featured a multimedia production incorporating props, stage lighting, a video, loud music, and pyrotechnics. After he researched it more he intended to write about the fifteen minutes of show that cost more than ten thousand dollars. Jodie sang again, and his heart stood still. She had a professional-quality voice. It amazed him that she wasn't in Nashville rather than playing in the local honky tonks around southern Oklahoma.

It was just after eleven o'clock when they reached the lot where Jodie's pickup was parked. Using the remote key she unlocked the doors, but instead of pitching the keys to Jimmy she opened the driver's side and crawled inside.

"Making a mistake there, aren't you?" He waited.

"Not tonight. I'm too wired to sleep, and you've got an article to write. You can do that on a laptop while I drive. We'll pull into a place that has an Internet hookup come daylight, and you can send it. We've got at least thirty hours, so we'll take turns. I'll get the first shift. You can do the second one."

"Jodie, you aren't superwoman. Your arm is broken."

"My wrist is broken. I could ride a bull if they'd let me. It's my free arm." She held it up. "I can drive with my right hand. Promise. Get in and go to work. You are about to experience the real thing that the crew was talking about when they said they followed the circuit."

"If you get tired . . ."

"I won't," she said.

He opened up his laptop. "Okay, then tell me again what it means to be seeded. I heard that word a lot when we were in the trailers this afternoon."

She started the engine and backed out, glad to be doing something other than sitting in the passenger's seat. Driving calmed her; always had. One time that neither of her parents knew about, she'd made the drive from Ft. Pierce to Denver alone, without stopping at a motel. It hadn't been wise but she'd been in one of her superman moods.

"Seeded means the rider is ranked among the top forty-five bull riders. He or she will go to the PBR's major league tour, a 30-city Built Ford Tough Series presented by Wrangler. The top forty-five bull riders who earn the most money in regular season PBR competition qualify to the season finale, the World Finals held in Las Vegas. The rider has to win enough money to maintain his ranking among the top forty-five riders or he risks being replaced by a rider who earns more money in the Challenger Tour."

"What's a Challenger Tour?"

"It's like a minor league baseball game. It gives up-and-coming riders a chance to compete in sanctioned events while they earn enough money to qualify them for the Tough Series."

He typed as she talked. "Just learning the lingo is a full-time job."

"What else?" she asked.

"Nothing right now. When you get tired, I can stop and take over."

It didn't happen until daybreak when she stopped at a Love's to refill the gas tank. She picked up two large coffees, a quart of milk, and a dozen Krispy Kreme doughnuts, using his credit card to pay for them, while he sent his article out to his editors.

"You too tired to drive a couple of hours?" she asked.

"I'm still wired after that story. God, I've never felt so alive," he admitted.

"We're just getting started," she said. "Doughnuts for both of us. Coffee for you. Milk for me."

"Decaf?"

"Hell, no. You need a jolt to stay awake while I catch a nap," she said.

"Why'd you buy two coffees then?"

"I'll drink the other one cold when I wake up."

He shuddered.

"You'll get the hang of it. By the time we get done, you'll be drinking it leftover from the day before and stone cold."

"I doubt it." He waited until he was back on the highway before he held out his hand for a pastry.

They finished the whole dozen, and she drained the last of the milk before she grabbed her pillow from the back seat and curled up against the window. In seconds she was sound asleep. He stole glances at her. She was the grown-up version of that little girl who'd taken up for him on Rodeo Day at the ranch. The little girl he'd been obsessed with for more than twenty years.

By mid-morning Jodie had just finished a four hour stint and nosed the truck into a parking space at a roadside rest. Jimmy had driven four hours that morning before his coffee, doughnuts, and energy played out. She'd taken over the wheel and made it on energy the first three. After that it was an hour on sheer raw nerves. She couldn't believe she'd ever made the trip without any sleep at all. Jimmy stirred and mumbled, but he didn't wake. She reached down and pushed the lever that laid the seat back, locked the doors, and shut her eyes.

A slow drizzle had started when Jimmy opened his eyes to find they were sitting still in a rest stop parking lot. So she wasn't superwoman after all. He checked the time and realized he'd been asleep six hours. "Hey, sleeping beauty," he whispered. "Wake up enough to slide over in this seat, and I'll drive."

"Mmmm," she mumbled and rolled toward him.

He barely had time to unlock and open the door before she claimed his side. He was already on the wet pavement when he remembered he'd taken his shoes off. He wasted no time getting around the truck and into the driver's seat.

"Yuck!" He snarled as he took off his cold, wet socks. The suitcase with dry ones was on the very bottom of the stack behind Jodie. He could drive barefoot but his feet were cold. He started to put his shoes on without socks but then he noticed that Jodie had removed both shoes and socks before she went to sleep. Her knees were tucked up under her and a hooded sweat shirt covered her feet. So what if her socks were hot pink trimmed in turquoise—they looked warm.

He drove through the rain, into the sunshine, nibbled on crackers he found in her sack for lunch, and kept driving. Talk about an education in the rodeo circuit; he was getting one first-hand. He had an idea and flipped open his cell phone to see if it was even a possibility. When Cathy answered he spoke softly, hoping that Jodie wouldn't wake at the sound of his voice.

Hours later, she awoke slowly, opening one eye and closing it. Then she opened both eyes and blinked several times to bring the clock on the dash into focus. She sat up with a start. "Good Lord, it's six. I've been asleep almost eight hours."

"Yes, you have. Hungry?"

"Starving. Did you get into my crackers? That's an

empty wrapper right there, and I know I didn't eat in my sleep."

"Yes, I did. And I borrowed your socks too. My feet were cold."

She smiled and his heart cranked in an extra beat.

"Where are we?"

"We got on Interstate 70 a while back. We'll probably make Denver by two or three in the morning. I've called ahead for reservations at a hotel, but I got an idea while you were asleep I want to run past you . . ."

"Huh-oh," she said.

"You can veto it. I'm having someone check about renting us a couple of trailers for the rest of the time we're in Denver. So is it a hotel or trailers?"

"Trailers."

"Okay, then I'll call and make it official," he said.

"Want me to drive?"

"I'm fine until after we eat." He pushed a few buttons and said a few words, then held the phone to his chest. "Problem, here. We can get a trailer from a rental place but there's a scarcity of lots. Can't find two together at an RV place. So it's hotel or share since we've only got one vehicle. Your call."

She fluttered her eyelids. "Are you asking me to live with you?"

"No ma'am, I most certainly am not!" he said coldly.

"Then it's a trailer." Her tone dripped with just as much ice.

"Cathy, honey, we'll take the single trailer. Rent the biggest one possible. And I owe you, darlin'. Book us a table at your favorite restaurant for when I get back," he said. "Okay, and a concert too. I'll be in touch."

"It'll be set up on the eleventh. We'll stay in the hotel until then," he said. *Is she always grumpy when she's hungry?* One minute she was flirtatious, the next chilly.

She watched the cold wintery scene speed past and didn't look at him. "Fine."

"What's your problem? If we're going to live together for almost two weeks, I need to know if this ugly mood is something that just jumps on you out of nowhere or is it something I've done?"

She thought about it for a minute. "I'm sorry. That was my fault. You hurt my feelings when you said you weren't asking me to live with you. It came out all cold and hateful. I shouldn't have taken it that way."

"So does that mean you want to live with me?" he asked.

"No, but one minute we were teasing and the next you were so definite. Do you have a girlfriend or a significant other back in . . . where do you live?"

"I do not have a significant other and at the present I'm not involved with any one woman," he said. Great Scot, he couldn't tell her that his comment had popped out because he was on this trip to get over her, not live with her. He wanted her out of his mind and his dreams. He didn't want to measure every woman in the world by what he thought Jodie Cahill had grown up to be. No, he didn't want to live with her for real, but he couldn't tell her why without giving away his whole life. And strong-willed Jodie would think he was totally pathetic if she knew that.

She almost smiled. "Okay, we got that out of the way. Evidently you get pretty crabby when you are hungry too. Either that or my pink socks don't agree with you. Hey, look at that sign. It says there's a Chili's at the next exit. You up for fajitas?"

"Yes, ma'am. And Jodie, when I'm not in the field, I live in San Antonio, Texas."

They checked into their hotel rooms at four A.M. and slept for twelve straight hours, waking in time for supper in the hotel restaurant before they were scheduled to be at Denver National Western every night for the next two weeks.

Chapter Three

"**S**o you want to drive four miles or ten miles from the RV park to the rodeo place?" he asked as they headed to the National Western Stockyards from the hotel. The air was thin and cold so he'd brought along his black overcoat, in spite of Jodie telling him he looked more like a mafia don than a man on his way to a bull riding competition.

"Folks I know stay at the Prospect. It's about ten miles out," she said.

He made a phone call and the deal was done. "Cathy is taking care of details. It'll be waiting for us tonight. She'll call back with instructions."

She motioned at the sign in front of them. "Turn right there. We're going to the coliseum parking lot."

His phone rang by the time he locked the truck doors. He stopped under a street light and wrote in his notebook. He was glad all he had to do was mutter because if he'd had to talk he would have been a stuttering, bumbling fool. The warm glow of yellow street lights provided a spotlight for Jodie. She'd dressed in electric blue that night. Tight-fitting pants, a lacy-looking blouse that flared at her wrists and a long, blue leather duster over the top of it all. Even the sling holding her left arm steady didn't look out of place on Jodie Cahill that night. All she needed was a microphone and she could be making a video for Country Music Television.

"We've got an RV on the way," he finally said. "This is a busy place."

"It's a hundred acres split diagonally by the Burlington Northern Railroad. The actual stockyards are on the other side of the tracks. Think of a smaller triangle within the larger one on this side. That's where most things are located: the events center, stadium and expo hall. The coliseum is outside the smaller triangle. I'm sure you've done your research and seen a map already though, haven't you? Here we are." She showed the ticket taker her pass and the two of them went inside. She'd barely found her seat in the judge's panel when the opening ceremonies began. Two nights before she'd been in Ft. Pierce and the show wasn't so different, but the music, lights, and excitement never ceased to thrill her.

From that point she focused on the rides: how well the rider kept up with the bull, how many points she could award the bull for his kicks and bucks. By the end of the evening she was wound up tighter than a neurotic whose therapist was on vacation.

As if on cue, Jimmy was there waiting. "Ready to go find our humble abode?"

"I'm ready but I'm not sleepy. I think I've got my nights and days turned around with all the driving and sleeping in the day time."

"Want to hit an all-night Wal-Mart store and pick up food for a few days? Cathy has taken care of bare essentials like toilet paper and dish soap, but I told her we'd do our own shopping."

"There's one on Smith Road not far from here. I'll direct. You drive. The traffic will be fierce since this is the last event for the day. Hey, did you pick up a schedule?"

"Printed one out before we left home. It's in my briefcase. Why?"

"Because we're at a stock show. For the next two weeks there's something going on every single hour of every day. Did you think we'd just go to the evening bull ride or the rodeo and go home to sit in a trailer? Not so, Mr. James Moses. I want to see it all."

"Even if it involves getting up early?"

"I'm a rancher. I get up early all the time."

They inched along in traffic until they got on Interstate 70, where she instructed him to catch Exit 278 and then turn left onto Smith Road. Wal-Mart was less than half a mile away.

She put bacon, sausage, eggs, peppers, onions, whole milk, two steaks, baking potatoes, and a package of sweet rolls in the cart. He added bananas, kiwi, skim milk, cans of soup, and mangoes. Together they chose whole wheat bread and smoked ham for sandwiches.

"I'm hungry. I had thought after the supper we ate I wouldn't want food until tomorrow evening at the earliest," he said.

"Supper was hours ago. I'll make omelets and steaks when we get to the trailer. It does have a stove, doesn't it?"

"No, Cathy got us a pup tent and we have to use a charcoal burner, but the outhouse is only a few feet away so you won't freeze to death when you have to get up in the middle of the night."

"*It* has a sense of humor," she said in awe.

"In my circles, I'm considered quite the funny guy," he said.

"Lord, I'd hate to run in your circles," she said.

"Doubt that you ever will."

"Are we fighting?" she asked.

"Seems we do pretty often. You sure you'll be able to handle nearly two weeks in the same trailer with humorless me?"

She put a case of Dr. Pepper in the cart. "Hey, I didn't mean to hurt your little feelings."

He put in a case of Diet Coke.

"No comebacks?" she asked.

"My feelings aren't hurt. We disagreed. We are adults, not kindergarteners. Is that all we need for this week?"

"No! It's all we need for tonight and maybe breakfast. When we see how big the refrigerator is in our pup tent, we'll buy more. Hey, look." She pointed toward a rack of Wrangler jeans. "Want to look like a cowboy the rest of the trip?"

"No!"

"Why?"

"I hate jeans. They're stiff and uncomfortable. I'd rather be a mafia don than a cowboy." He didn't tell her that the only time he'd worn jeans was back in kindergarten when he visited the Cahill ranch. Or that everything that happened on that day had caused him to blame jeans and a little red Western shirt with pearl snaps.

She pushed the cart toward the checkout counter. "Just as well. Your tasseled shoes wouldn't go with Wranglers anyway."

"What's wrong with my shoes?" he asked.

"Not one thing. They match your mafia outfits just fine."

"Okay. Bit of history. Except for a couple of days when I was a little kid, I attended private school where dress slacks and blazers were the uniform. Unlike someone who grew up on a ranch or in a place like Sulphur, Oklahoma, I wasn't put into denim the day I could walk."

She bit back a smile. "I see. Now I understand your whole life perfectly. Except this Cathy woman who runs your life for you. Who is she?"

"Stop being cranky. We'll get that monster fed soon. And Cathy? Well, you are right, she's the woman who runs my life for me," he said.

The cashier looked up as she scanned the items. "My husband says when I'm hungry no one, not even Jesus Christ, could live with me."

"I understand," Jimmy said.

But he didn't stutter, stammer, and blubber around denying that Jodie was his wife. She found that rather amusing.

When they reached the RV park he drove slowly between lots until he found the right one, parked the truck in the allotted space, and picked up four grocery bags to carry inside.

Jodie sat in stunned silence. Surely he'd made a mistake. That tour bus couldn't be what he'd rented. It would cost more than a five-star hotel. She watched as he lifted a key from between the two doors and went inside. She finally picked up one bag with her right hand and carried it inside.

The RV was at least thirty feet long. She'd walked into the kitchen/living area. Two off-white leather swivel chairs flanked a small kitchen table. Plenty of cabinets to hold their groceries, a microwave, in addition to a stove with four burners and an oven, a refrigerator, and even a small stackable washer and dryer were tucked into the kitchen area. Two sofas lined the long sides of the narrow living room; one made out into a bed. And beyond that was a real bedroom with a queen-sized bed, a dresser complete with mirror, a bathroom with a shower and sheer draperies over the windows. Everything was in shades of brown to complement the sandy-colored carpet. Jodie was in love.

"This is someone's tour bus. Do you have a friend who's a star or something?"

"No, I have a very large expense account. I'll live in cheap hotels and check out of good ones early so I can get the feel for the circuit, but when I'm staying in a place for two weeks, I think we need some luxuries. You can have the bedroom. I'll sleep on the couch. You have to pay, though. I get to shower first every night so that I can get to work faster. Also I get to unpack my things in half the closet space, and I'm claiming half the drawers in the dresser. Oh, and I get half the medicine cabinet for my shaving equipment."

"Small price," she said.

"I'm still hungry and I think you promised me an omelet. Think you could get it done by the time I take a shower?"

"Depends on how long you take. I won't keep it hot so you'd better hurry or you'll be eating cold omelet."

"Then I'll shower after we eat. I'll bring in the rest of the baggage while you cook. I believe Cathy had it outfitted with everything we need. Kitchen stuff. Towels. Sheets."

Jodie nodded, still amazed. She went to work putting away the groceries they'd bought and getting acquainted with the kitchen. By the time he had the truck unloaded she'd made a western omelet and toast. He left his unpacking to do later and set the table for two while she buttered the toast.

He laid a stapled stack of printed papers on the table between them. "And here is the schedule you asked about. This smells wonderful."

She picked up the schedule and ran a finger down the next day's events. "Hope you like onions."

"Love them."

She blew on a fork full of eggs until they stopped steaming and looked over the papers. "Aha."

"What?"

"The Dress Western Barbecue Lunch is tomorrow at eleven-thirty. I want to do that. It's on Seventeenth and Broadway downtown at the Wells Fargo Atrium and the parade comes down Seventeenth at noon, so we'll be right there. They'll have marching bands and the longhorn cattle drive."

"This is wonderful. Are you a cook or is this your only skill?"

"I can cook."

"More than omelet and bologna sandwiches."

"Boy, I could fatten you up in six months to where all

you'd ever want to wear would be bibbed overalls with the top buttons undone," she said.

He smiled and those wrinkle-dimples deepened. He was handsome in his own way, she guessed. Not as rugged as Chris, her old flame, but not ugly by any means. He'd do to sit across the table with for breakfast for a few weeks. Especially when she could spend the time in a place like this.

They shared clean-up, careful to stay out of each other's way. He went to the bedroom to unpack and have a shower. She pulled out her cell phone and called her sister. Rosy sounded groggy when she answered, which caused Jodie to look at the microwave clock.

"It's me. I'm so sorry. I didn't realize it was so late. I'm wired for sound and forgot that you'd be asleep," she said.

"Anything the matter? Your arm hurting? Something important going on? Did you marry that good-looking hunk you're traveling with?"

"None of the above."

"Then call me at a decent hour and learn to check the time."

Jodie had barely hung up the phone when a gentle knock took her attention to the door. She wondered who'd come calling after midnight but wasn't surprised when she found an old friend, Laney, on the other side.

"Hey girl, I saw your truck. I'd recognize that bumper sticker anywhere. You up for a while?"

Jodie swung the door open and hugged Laney. "I'm so glad you're here. Want some Dr. Pepper or a Coke?"

Laney looked around at the interior of the RV. "Wow! Did you win the lottery or rob a bank?"

"Neither. It's called a big expense account," Jodie said.

"Well, I'm going to start judging instead of riding them bulls if it means getting a sweet little deal like this. Yes, I'll have a Coke."

"Have to be on ice. They're warm."

"That's fine," Laney said. "Did you get married?" she whispered.

"Hell, no!" Jodie blushed.

"Then . . ."

Jodie called into the bedroom. "Jimmy, come and meet my friend and rival when I can ride."

He'd already unbuttoned his shirt and only fastened the middle one as he came out of the bedroom.

"Hello," he said.

"This is James Moses Crowe, a writer who's covering the circuit and some rodeo events the next few months. We're traveling together so I can answer his questions."

He held out his hand. "Please call me Jimmy."

She looked directly into his eyes without blinking. "I will and often."

"I'll get back to my shower so you ladies can visit," he said.

"Sure you're in a hurry?" Laney came on strong but that was her style.

"I've got several hours of work before I can call it a night," he explained.

Laney smiled that brilliant way that brought most men crawling to her on their knees. "Then next time."

"Nice to meet you," he threw a towel over his shoulder as he closed the bedroom door.

Laney picked up the schedule pages and fanned herself. "Please tell me you are living with him in a purely platonic relationship. I haven't seen anything that pretty in a very long time. He's got dimples like Matthew Mc-Conaughey. I think I'm already in love."

"Good grief, girl. Those are early wrinkles, not dimples. Get out the Visine. You've been up too long or else you've still got arena dust in your eyes," Jodie said.

"Does that mean he's off limits?"

"That means he's got a girlfriend named Cathy in Texas," she said.

Laney pressed her hand against her chest. "I am hurt. My heart is dying. I may never be able to ride again."

"Not until you see a pair of tight-fittin' Wranglers and a Kevlar vest. He's not our type, Laney. He's a citified dandy who wears tassels on his shoes."

"Honey, with those eyes and curls I don't care what he wears," Laney declared.

Jodie deliberately changed the subject. "Enough about my roommate. You didn't give your ride tonight a hundred percent. With that Arizona chick coming up the ranks you can't afford to lose points. What was the matter?"

"Chris."

A feeling of déjà vu hit Jodie in the pit of her stomach. "Chris who?"

"Is there two of them floating around? I've been seeing him for three months. That's why I didn't call the last while. Didn't want to tell you. Either you'd scream and yell about him being a jackass or else you'd cry. I didn't want to hear either one."

Jodie held her breath. "What happened?"

"Same old thing that's been happening for five years. He gets all involved and then he backs off. Flowers. Calling every night to say good night. Then cold feet. Isn't that what happened with you?"

"No. I wanted something different than he did. He wanted to run the circuit until he was too old to get on a bull. I wanted to stop sometime in the future and raise a family on a ranch, preferably in Murray County, Oklahoma. It was a dead end so I put an end to it."

"Did you forget him overnight?"

"No. Sometimes I still think about the good night calls and flowers. Never got to the cold feet," Jodie said.

"We had a big fight. He hasn't changed. Still loves the circuit and doesn't care if he barely makes enough money to last from one ride to the next. I wanted a commitment even if it wasn't the ranch with a bunch of little mutton busters running around. He's riding tomorrow night. How are you going to judge him fairly? What happens if he thinks you are prejudiced?"

"Hey, don't worry about me. How long have you wallowed around in this pity pool?"

"More than fifteen minutes. If that pretty thing back there in the shower didn't already have a woman, I'd make a play for him," Laney said.

"Go find another pretty thing. There are lots of them around this place." Jodie didn't know why she even cared. She tried to convince herself right then that it was because she didn't want Laney to get hurt.

"I'll take a look around but it won't do any good. I'm smitten with Chris and even the Matty look-alike probably wouldn't take my mind off him."

"Whether you get your mind off him or not, you've got to stop thinking about him for the eight seconds you're on that bull," Jodie said.

"Don't I know it. I almost lost it tonight when old Red Bones rolled. I just about grabbed the bull rope with my free hand before I got it under control. It's a wonder I wasn't disqualified. Tell me, what critter tossed you hard enough to break your arm? I missed the Lexington ride. Was it there?"

"I fell on a patch of ice," Jodie shrugged.

Laney laughed hard enough that tears ran through her mascara and dripped black streaks down her cheeks.

She wiped them away with the back of her hand. "I can't believe it. You've never even gotten a broken bone or stitches while riding and you fall on ice. That's rich. I can't wait to tell everyone. We've been taking bets on which critter threw you and hoping like hell we didn't get him in the draw."

Jodie laughed with her. "Unless his name is Ice, you ain't got a thing to worry about."

"I'm going home. If Matty breaks up with his woman, call me. Don't matter where I am or what time it is. I think he could make me forget all about Chris," Laney stood up. She was just over five feet tall, small-waisted, round-hipped, with a bosom that might not put Dolly Parton to shame but wouldn't lack a lot. Most men tumbled all over themselves when she blinked twice at them.

"Keep me posted. And ride better tomorrow night." Jodie followed her to the door and locked it behind her.

Laney just nodded and disappeared into the trailer next door.

Jimmy poked his head out of the bedroom. "Is she gone?"

"Just barely. I'm ready for a shower. You got your things unpacked?"

Jimmy carried his laptop out to the kitchen table and set up shop. "It's all yours. Will she be coming around often?"

"Probably. She's parked next door, and she's been my friend for years." Jodie didn't tell him that Laney was having man troubles.

"She was hitting on me," he said flatly.

"Scare you?"

"To death." He hoped that came out like a joke instead of fear.

"Yeah, right." She left him sitting at the table in pajama bottoms and a loose-fitting T-shirt.

He was teasing, wasn't he? she asked herself as she hung up her fancy lace blouse. Tomorrow night she'd wear the black and the one after that the red. Then she'd rotate the outfits again.

She went to sleep at dawn still unsure about James's comment.

Chapter Four

Jimmy sat across the table from Jodie at the Wells Fargo Atrium eating the best barbecue he'd had in years. He'd eat a few bites and take a dozen pictures, then repeat the process. He'd taken several shots of the lobby where a golden aura surrounded Jodie. Criss-crossed latticework covered the ceiling and a yellow glow from the side lighting worked together to set her into what appeared to be the golden courts of heaven. She wore jeans and a white flowing blouse with billowing sleeves that didn't pose a problem with her cast. He caught her just as she looked up and the picture came out as if he'd used a sepia filter on an old 35 millimeter camera.

They certainly didn't have to elbow for room as they stood on the street and waited for the parade to begin.

Jimmy began to think the whole thing was overrated. Perhaps it was the snow keeping the people inside because the only folks he could see anywhere were a bunch of bundled up photographers with everything from big old-fashioned cameras to expensive digitals like he used. Those toting photographic equipment outnumbered the spectators two to one easily.

Snowflakes as big as quarters floated down and lay gently on the fur around Jodie's parka hood. He took a few shots of her, careful to catch her when she wasn't paying attention. The crowd began to grow as the parade progressed. People came out of the buildings where they'd been working or keeping warm and watched the marching bands strut their stuff; fancy-dressed cowboys and cowgirls rode spirited horses, their breath coming out in puffs of smoke in the cold air; wagons pulled by teams of Belgians to bring back the memories of the old days before automobiles took normal precedence on Seventeenth Street.

The circus figures entertained the crowd. Jimmy took pictures of the man on stilts and two Shetland sheepdogs pulling a tiny chuck wagon. Clowns were everywhere: round ones, tall ones, colorful ones, black-and-white monochromatic ones. Jimmy got a picture of a clown blowing Jodie a kiss.

Then the longhorned steers brought their version of noise as they charged up the street, reminding Jimmy of the famous "running of the bulls" in Spain. From bellowing bulls of every description to sassy rodeo queens in their sequins and glitter to heart-thumping band music—it was all overwhelming. He could understand why Jodie had insisted they come to town to see it all. And the pictures: they were going to be such an addition to tonight's story.

The ones of Jodie he'd download into a special file.

A fierce wind blew Jodie's parka off her left shoulder, and Jimmy reached up and tucked it back around her. Using her right arm she tugged it across her chest. She'd learned to dress herself with one arm, could even pull up her slacks, fasten them, and button her shirts, but it was nice to have a little help.

"Thanks," she said.

He nodded. "We've got fifteen minutes to get to this lowlife sale you wanted to attend. Ready?"

"Lowline, not lowlife," she said.

"All the same to me. The only way I know one breed from the other is if someone tells me. I could probably pick out a longhorn though," he said.

She rolled her eyes. "You'd be as helpful as Trey on a ranch."

"And Trey is?"

"Roseanna's husband. He's a city slicker deluxe. Although I'll have to give credit where it's due. He did help me pull a calf and did a fine job. You think you could do that? Pull a calf?"

They'd reached the place where he'd parked the truck that morning. At least the snow was dry and could be swept away by the windshield wipers. Had it been wet, he'd have been doing some major scrapping. Already there was an inch blowing in circles around their feet on the sidewalk. For a minute he wished he did own a pair of boots. Dress shoes and nylon socks were failing to keep his feet warm.

"What did you say? My mind was elsewhere. I heard that Trey is your sister's husband. But what about pulling a calf? What do you mean?"

"I mean put a rope around it and pull it out of its momma," she said.

He tried to keep a straight face but his nose twitched.

"You are serious. You've never heard of pulling a calf?"

"I've lived in the city my whole life except for a very short while when we lived in a small town. So no, I don't know a thing about pulling a calf." His voice held a razor-sharp edge.

"Don't get snappy with me. I can see where you'd need help if you've only lived in the city. You could have covered the circuit, but your stories wouldn't have had much life. We're going to the livestock center auction arena. That'll be across the tracks. You can see what it's like over there in the historical side of things."

"Don't get all preachy to me. I looked on the map before we left this morning. I know where to go. I'm not stupid just because I haven't pulled a calf or driven one of your tractors. If you were in the city you'd be out of your element just as much as I am in the country."

"Bet me."

"How much?"

"Don't play with the big dogs, James Moses. I could whoop you in the city or on the farm," she said.

"Don't call me James Moses."

"Then don't get all defensive when I tell you something. Your momma sure named you right. I think Moses argued with God Himself a few times."

"My grandmother named me, thank you very much. We'll be in San Antonio for two weeks. We'll stay at my place and . . ."

"And I'll be busy doing the stock show and rodeo, just like here," she interrupted.

"Not every waking minute. So we'll see how you like my town with my friends who wear tassels on their shoes," he said.

The corners of her mouth quivered as she kept back the grin. He didn't know the Cahill girls very well but he was about to learn.

"Okay, but it's my world now and I really want to see what kind of price these Lowline cattle are bringing. I'm thinking of buying some to put on my own place if and when I save enough money to buy a few acres of my very own."

They bent their heads against the wind, waded across frozen dirt and cow droppings to the auction area.

"Why on earth would anyone have a livestock show at this time of year?" he grumbled as they found seats in the arena.

"Because that's the only time of the year when the ranching industry slows down enough to take a few days off. Put this in the middle of spring and it couldn't draw near the crowd. In the summer, ranchers are too busy to get away for two weeks. Daddy tells that when my great-great-grandfather came to this show it was held in the open stockyards or under a canvas tent. He said he dang near froze to death. One year the snow was so deep it got in over the top of his boots, but he didn't care. Cold feet were worth enduring to be able to talk to all the major cattle operations in the country. He got a lot of good advice and gave just as much, I'm sure. In those days the cowhands slept in their cattle pens and the cattle were paraded down an alley to be judged. Story has it that he considered it the same as a family reunion." She looked around. "The sale is starting now. Keep your hands down or you might be bidding on a Lowline to take home with you, and they don't do too well in an apartment."

He took out his notebook and pen. "You are just full of information."

She stuck her tongue out at him and turned her attention to the sale.

He wrote *Lowline* and underlined it. Whether he mentioned anything about it in his story he intended to find out just what kind of cattle Jodie wanted. The first black bovine led out into the ring didn't look all that different from the cows he'd seen at the Cahill ranch. The auctioneer gave the animal's history: a full blood open heifer named Miss Tallulah 2S. Sire: Montezuma. Dam: Tallulah 018S. Consignor: Low Water Ranch, Colorado Springs, Colorado.

The auctioneer began a fast rattle and hands went up. He caught his breath and began again. More hands. More bids. Jimmy could scarcely believe a chunk of hamburger on the hoof could bring that much money. Finally a bidder from Bennington, Oklahoma, purchased the cow for $9,900.

"What makes a cow worth that?" he asked Jodie.

"Lowlines were derived from pure Aberdeen Angus bloodlines in Australia. There was a lot of research done but the short story is that they figured out a very impressive conversion of grass-to-meat ratios within the breed. The herd was closed until 1993 when a complete sale was made of 20 bulls, 44 cows, and 51 heifers. That was the foundation stock of the American Lowlines."

"You know your history, but why would you want these rather than those other black cows on Cahill ranch? What makes the difference?" he asked.

"They're docile and easy to handle. They make wonderful animals for children to handle and show. Plus, you've got to grow your cattle for the market. These are smaller than Angus so they have a smaller carcass which produces smaller cuts of meat. They'll mature on grass alone, which means you save money on grain. From what I read on them, tests proved that the meat is tender and tasty and the test stock had been fed on grass and hay alone. And grass-fed beef is healthier than grain-fed. It's got more vitamins, more CLA which fights cancer and less fatty acids. Last, since they're smaller, I could put more cattle per acre."

"Well, stop the show, we'll buy everything they've got," he said.

She shook her finger at him. "Don't tease me about something near and dear to my old heart. This is my dream. Besides darlin', unless you own Fort Knox, you couldn't buy them all. A couple of years ago the Lowline sale had less than a hundred head and the total sales came in at just under half a million."

"Dollars?" He raised an eyebrow.

"Not nickels!"

"Okay, ladies and gentlemen, we've got seven bred females here." The auctioneer went on with the pedigree and then started the bidding. When he slapped the gavel down, the lot had brought $68,000.

It was mid-afternoon by the time they stepped out into the blustery wind and snow again. It shifted across the frozen earth to drift against buildings. Already the

drifts were a foot tall. And Jimmy had a whole new respect for Lowline cattle.

"What now?" Jimmy asked.

"First we go to the trade show and see if we can buy
you some gloves. Didn't you know it got cold in Denver? Then we're going to find a vendor and have some
funnel cakes and whatever else looks good."

"Want to drive?"

"No, it's not that far. Walk fast and keep your hands
in your pockets."

"Where are we going to buy gloves again?" he asked.

"You can find anything here from portable sheds to
boots. The tradeshow opens at nine every morning and
closes at eight at night. There're all kinds of booths in
several buildings but we're going to the expo hall. That's
where I expect we'll find what we're looking for. By the
time we eat it'll be time to go home and get ready for
the bull ride tonight." She grimaced at the thought of
having to judge Chris's ride, but Jimmy had his head
down and didn't see it.

The booth selling leather products had gloves, vests,
hats, boots, and even leather-bound picture frames and
albums for sale. Jimmy tried on gloves until he found a
fur-lined pair he liked. He wished aloud for fur-lined
socks to keep his feet warm.

"Try on a pair of boots. They don't have to be fancy
eel or have pointed toes, you know. They can actually

look more like shoes with your pants legs shook down over them," she said.

"What's the advantage? Do they eat less grass than my loafers and produce better meat?"

"You can wear good warm wool socks with boots and no one knows," she told him.

"Aha, they do have an advantage," he said.

The vendor held up a package of gray socks with red heels. "Six pair for fifteen dollars."

"Do you have a pair of plain boots in size ten?"

Jodie shuffled through several boot boxes and came up with a pair. "Right here. Try them on, but not with those thin socks. We'll take that package of socks whether the boots fit or not so can we open them now?"

The vendor pulled a pair out for them.

The boots actually felt pretty good with the socks and his feet were already warmer.

"Want to wear them?" the vendor asked.

"Sure," Jimmy answered.

While he put his shoes in the boot box and paid the man, Jodie slipped on a long leather duster made with wide arms and fringe hanging from the sleeves. It fit over the cast comfortably. It would be perfect in the cold weather. She wouldn't have to drape the left side of her other jackets and coats over her shoulder. She checked the price tag and came close to having a full-fledged cardiac arrest on the spot.

"Want it?" the vendor asked.

"I could buy a calf for the price of that thing," she said.

"I could reduce the price some since your husband bought boots and gloves," he said.

"How much?"

"A hundred dollars."

"He bought socks and he's looking at that trifold wallet," she said.

"Hey, don't rope me into this," Jimmy said.

"How much if he buys the wallet?"

"Half off," the vendor smiled.

"You're buying the wallet," she said, reaching in her purse for her credit card.

"But I don't need it," he said.

"Then give it to Paul for Christmas or one of your city friends for Christmas."

The vendor laughed. "You two been married long?"

Jodie signed her name on the line. "No, sir."

"I didn't think so. You haven't even changed your name on your cards yet. You make a cute couple," he said.

Jimmy blushed scarlet, the creases of his dimples looking pale in comparison. "Thank you. I'll take two of these wallets."

"Why'd you buy two?" she asked when they were out of the vendor's hearing.

"They'll make good gifts. Besides, he gave you a good deal on the coat," Jimmy answered.

"Oh, I thought you were just being a good husband," she teased.

"I will be someday to someone," he said, leaving no doubt that it wouldn't be today or Jodie.

Jodie was glad she hadn't been asked to sing that night. She still worried about being totally fair when she judged Chris and Laney. By the time the chute opened with the first rider on the back of Blue Devil, a twisting ton of bull hailing from West Texas, she forgot all about fairness or who was riding. She watched for turns, bucks, the rider's free hand and his form.

Chris rode his eight seconds and raised both hands in his traditional victory sign. She and the other judge handed in their score sheets, and the next rider took his turn. He lasted almost four seconds before he landed on his hind end in a puff of dirt. Laney did better that night than the previous one. Jodie was jealous that she had to sit in the judge's panel and couldn't ride.

The event was over before eleven and a whole crowd gathered around her. Laney was the first to ask if she'd join them at the IHOP for breakfast and talk. There was just one more night of the bull rides and several of them would be leaving immediately after Wednesday night so they could make the Pueblo U.S. Smokeless Tobacco Challenger Tour at the Colorado State Fair Event Center. Jodie had hoped she'd be listed as a judge for that tour but the schedule they'd given her and Jimmy kept them in Denver for the whole National Western affair. Her job would continue right on, judging bull riding every evening. The point system was a little different but the rules were the same. The only advantage was that she'd be finished earlier, and could watch the roping, steer wrestling, barrel racing, and other events.

"So what do you say? Can you go, or do you have to hold the mafia don's hand while he writes his cute little stories?" Laney asked.

"She can go. I don't need anyone to hold my hand," Jimmy said from right behind Laney.

She slapped her hand over her mouth. "Ooops!"

"Call me when you get ready to come home, and I'll drive over and get you." Jimmy waved at her.

"Oooooh," Laney whistled under her breath. "He's going to be all alone in that fancy trailer. Maybe I'll go keep him company and make him forget Pollyanna back at home."

Jodie laced her good arm through Laney's. "Come on darlin'. You know we always share everything on our plates. Who'll give me bites of blueberry pancakes if you don't order them?"

Laney forgot about Jimmy for the time being. "And who'll let me have half her gravy?"

A group of twenty took up several tables and visited back and forth to talk about the results of the rides and who was in the lead and who might upstage them from the Challenger Tour. The year was just beginning and it was a long time and many miles until the finals in Las Vegas but they could make their five-dollar bets.

"I don't know why ya'll even bother betting," Chris said. "It's my buckle this year. What do you say, Jodie? Give me a few extra points in the Oklahoma City ride?"

"I'm a fair judge. You'll get what you earn, and I'm not doing the Oklahoma City show this circuit," she said.

One of the ladies fanned herself. "Whooo! Is that the way you operate in all things, Jodie? Get what you earn?"

"No, she don't even give a feller what he earns most of the time," Chris taunted.

"If you're making this personal, let me in on the conversation," Laney said.

Jodie held up a hand. "Let's don't throw ice water on a good time. So who's riding tomorrow night?"

It was two in the morning before she and Laney went home.

Laney nosed her truck into the parking spot beside her personal trailer. Tomorrow she would hook it onto the truck and be ready to pull out for Pueblo as soon as the lights went out in the coliseum.

Laney yawned without even covering her mouth with her hand. "God, I'm so tired I could sleep on a concrete mattress. Want me to walk you home?"

"No, it's right next door. I can see the lights from here. Sleep tight and thanks for the ride."

"You are welcome," Laney said.

Jodie was about to open the door when a big masculine hand covered hers.

"A minute of your time, please ma'am," Chris said.

"Since you said *please* you can have one minute. Any more and you'll be talking to a sleeping lump," she said.

He kept her hand in his and pulled her down to sit beside him on the step, snow blowing all around them. "I was teasing back there. I just wanted you to know that. I didn't mean anything personal."

She removed her hand from his and tucked it inside her pocket. "Okay."

"And I want to know if there's a chance for us to get back together. I know that would be a conflict of interest for you to judge me if we did. It's not that I've got ulterior motives. I believe you are fair," he stammered around the issue.

"I don't think there is a chance of it, Chris. We still want different things and it would be a waste of time."

"You mean you're not ready to give up all that silliness about kids and a ranch? I thought because you were back on the circuit you'd figured out what was important to you," he said.

She took a long look at him. Dark hair. Muscles in all the right places. Same general interests that she had. She felt nothing. Not one blessed tinge of excitement. "I'm sorry, Chris. It won't work. I'm just here to do a little judging during the slow time at the ranch. I'd hoped to make enough on this circuit to buy a small start but then I broke my arm. I wasn't taking the way things turned out very well and when the offer came to judge, I took it, thinking maybe I'd get out of my funk."

"You absolutely sure about this? I mean this is it, Jodie. There won't be another chance."

"I'm very, very sure," she said.

"Then I'm going to see Laney and make up with her. She'll do what I want," he said.

"Don't try to make me jealous," she said.

Before she could blink the snowflakes from her eyelashes, he'd pulled her into his arms and kissed her passionately. His lips were cool. He wasn't doing a bad job. She just wanted it to be over.

The door opened in the middle of the kiss and light lit them up like the topper on a Christmas tree.

She pulled away.

Chris chuckled.

Jimmy just stood there.

Chris ignored Jimmy. "Change your mind?"

"No."

"Then *adios señorita*. May you have a long life on your ranch with all those mutton busters running around at your feet. When you read about me wearing that fifty thousand dollar gold buckle, remember that you could have shared my glory like I did yours back when you got it."

"Be happy and be safe," she said.

Jimmy had returned to the table by the time she went inside the house. "Who was that?" He tried to keep his tone noncommittal but it came out edgy.

"It was an old boyfriend. I was dating him when I

won the finals. He wanted to know if we could get back together. I told him no." She wondered why she was explaining this to Jimmy. It wasn't a bit of his business. They were colleagues of a sort, not even roommates.

Jimmy didn't know he was holding his breath until he let it out, covering his blunder with a cough. "Oh, well, did you have a good time?"

"Wonderful. Did you find something to eat?"

"I made a smoothie and had some graham crackers."

"Yuck! That's not food."

Jimmy smiled.

Her heart did a fast two-step. "What's your angle tonight?"

"The clowns, along with the normal, old dry stuff about who got how many points, who was ahead at the end of the night, and who might make it to the finals," he said.

"That's not dry. That's the life of a rider," she said. "You learn to write that in words that make someone feel like they're sitting there breathing the dust and holding their breath for eight seconds, hoping their rider makes it to the bell. Then you'll be a really good rodeo writer."

"You mean I'm not now?" he asked.

"Put your heart into it, Jimmy. You can give your readers a taste of real rodeo if your heart is in it. If it's not, the words are just words. Cold as your feet were without the socks and boots."

"Did his kiss make you all philosophical?"

"No, it bored me. You know why Sawyer Carver is the best rodeo writer in the world?"

"I'm sure you are about to tell me," he said coolly.

"Because he puts his readers in the arena. They can almost feel that old bull bucking them. Write about the clowns if you want, but give them bull riding first and foremost."

"Or what?"

"Or go home and write about something you love."

I can't write about Jodie Cahill. You're not riding and if you were then Sawyer would be writing about you.

"Good advice. I'm going to revise my story. Would you read it before I send it?"

"I'd be glad to but I'm not a writer. I just know what I want to read."

His deep-green eyes twinkled. So the kiss had bored her, had it? Maybe someday she'd see if one of his was boring.

Chapter Five

Jodie threw herself across the hotel bed, glad that Jimmy's room was at the end of the hall and not connected to hers. For the remainder of what was left of that day and the next she intended to do nothing but read, sleep, and try to make sense of the unrest in her heart. It wasn't upheaval or even turmoil, just an antsy feeling that something wasn't right. She hadn't called home in three days—maybe there was something wrong there.

"No," she whispered. "Rosy would call immediately if anyone was sick or there was a big family problem. It's not that."

She sighed deeply when her cell phone rang. It had to be Jimmy. What she really needed was two days totally away from the man; not living ten hotel doors away with easy phone access. She'd only seen him thirty minutes ago. Why would he be calling her already?

"Hello," she grumbled.

"Did you get up on the wrong side of the bed?" her grandmother asked.

"Granny, I thought you were someone else. No, I am not grumpy; at least not with you. Please tell me everything is all right at home. I've got this weird feeling."

"Everything is fine at home. But we've been making lots of decisions, and I need your input. Do you ever intend to take over the lodge?"

"Good grief. Where did that come from? You aren't sick, are you?" Jodie's blood ran cold. Granny Etta had been as big an influence in her upbringing as her mother and father. A strong-willed, determined lady, she'd taught them all responsibility through working at the lodge from the time they were big enough to see over a kitchen counter. The mere thought of her not being there was enough to make Jodie physically ill.

"No, I'm not sick. Never been better, matter of fact, but I am ready to retire. Something has come up in the family and I'm about to make an offer to your oldest sister, Melanie. Jim lost his job this week. You and Rosy live on the ranch here and I felt like I needed to ask you first, but I want to give them the lodge to run. Their daughters could be raised here like you girls were and . . ."

"Granny, you are preaching to the choir. If Jim and Melanie will take over the lodge, that's wonderful. It'll bring them back close where we can see them all the time. What did Rosy say?"

"Rosy has a new iron in the fire but she'll tell you. I'm not spilling beans there."

Jodie held her breath. "Is she pregnant?"

"I'm not telling the secret. But no, she's not pregnant. How about you? I heard that feller you're keeping company with is a fine-looking young man. Anything going on there?" Etta deftly changed the subject.

"I'm not telling but no," Jodie said.

Granny Etta chuckled. "I'll be living at the lodge when I'm home. At least until I decide what I want to do. Roxie wants me to move in with her. I may do it."

"You two would be wonderful roommates. You're together ninety percent of the time anyway, but give it some time and thought. You've been at that lodge so long it'd be like losing an old friend if you move out. You'd be lost but you could try it and come back home if it doesn't work out," Jodie said.

"From the mouths of babes. I'll think on it. I've got to call Melanie. Keep me posted, especially if there's anything to report on the romance line."

"Keep dreaming."

"I can hope," Etta said before she said good-bye and hung up.

Jodie tossed the phone to the other side of the

king-sized bed and laced her hands behind her head. Was she homesick? Maybe, but it didn't feel like home-sickness. She'd been on the road many times and had never felt like this. She couldn't describe it, wasn't sure she wanted to face the consequences if she did. Granny Etta used to tell her not to ask a question if she didn't want the answer, so she wasn't going to delve into it. Not today. Today she was going to shut her eyes, take a nice long nap and then go judge the bull riding at the PRCA Championship Rodeo. Tomorrow she planned to sleep late, read a good book, or watch television, judge again that night, and come right back to the hotel. She needed these two days to unwind and get ready for a stint in San Antonio. Thinking of the two days before the fair with Jimmy on his turf brought on even crazier feelings. Her eyes wouldn't shut and her mind refused to stop running. So she reached for the phone and called her sister Rosy.

"Hey, lady, it's snowing in Lincoln and colder than an Alaskan well-digger's belt buckle. Tell me what this great news is Granny Etta won't share," she said when Rosy answered.

"So she called. Are you okay with her giving the lodge to Melanie?"

"Hey, I'm elated. Now we just have to find a job for Vicky and Matt and we'll have the whole family back in Murray County," Jodie answered.

"What'd she tell you about my news?"

"Not one blessed thing except that you aren't pregnant," Jodie said.

Rosy laughed. "Not yet, but hopefully it will happen soon. My news is this: I've been approached by one of those government agencies with initials to work for them. I'd be on a consulting basis and teaching once a year for about six weeks right here in Sulphur."

"Wow, that's great. Are you going to do it?"

"Probably. I'll only have to be away from home when there's an emergency. Mostly they'll send the recruits to me for intense training. I'll teach them to follow trails in the woods as well as in the city. They've already asked to book the lodge for six weeks, and I'd be teaching here on the ranch."

"How's Trey with that?"

"He thinks it's wonderful. He says it's a talent."

"He's right. Hate to admit that he's right about anything, but it is a talent. You can weed out the ones who couldn't find their hind ends with both hands and a flashlight," Jodie said.

"That sounds like what they said only in more technical terms. They're interested in the ones with natural ability. The ones who don't make it will go into another field. Now tell me about you. You've had two weeks with Jimmy. What's up?"

"Nothing," Jodie said.

"Would you tell me if there was?"

"Probably not," Jodie answered.

"Call me when you change your mind?"

"Will do but I expect I'll call before that because hell will have to freeze over before I change my mind about Jimmy. He's very secretive. Not much can happen through a closed door. Not that I'd want it to anyway. He's sure not my type. More Greta's." Jodie tried to be flippant. It came out flat.

"Methinks my sister doth protest too much," Rosy said.

"And methinks all four of you with new husbands have weddings on the brain," Jodie said.

"Greta's type is Kyle. It just took her a while to figure it out and we do have weddings on the brain. We hope you can join us before you start drawing social security."

"I'm only twenty-six," Jodie protested.

"Tick-tock, tick-tock. Hear that. It's time running out," Rosy teased.

"I'm going to hang up now. Good-bye."

Jodie didn't find a thing funny in her sister's good-natured ribbing. All she wanted to do was take a nap and forget about James Moses Crowe for a little while. And Rosy had put her thoughts right back on him. Why did that man keep his life so close to his heart and refuse to share even little bits of it? She knew there was someone named Cathy who made reservations and took care of business for him. Was she a middle-aged secretary or much, much more? Then there was his friend,

Paul, who knew all his secrets so well he deemed himself Jimmy's therapist. She'd heard him talk to Cathy on the phone but only about business. She'd never actually heard a conversation between him and Paul.

Turn the tables though, and he'd overheard her talking to her family more than once. He knew she had three sisters and her grandmother ran a bed-and-board place called Cahill Lodge. It wasn't fair.

To top it all, her arm felt like it had a family of fire ants living under the cast. Twice now she'd actually scratched the cast and broken a fingernail. She needed something long and skinny to scratch with. She looked through her suitcase and found nothing. Opened the desk drawer; it was empty. Went on to the dresser drawers and right there in the last one, slid all the way to the back was a plastic fly swatter. She grabbed it up like a long-lost sister. Holding the business end of the swatter, she stuck the handle down inside the cast and carefully relieved the horrible itch. Three more weeks to go. Right after the stint in San Antonio she could go to the rodeo doctor and have the thing removed. It wouldn't be a day too soon either. She was sick of not having two healthy arms. She was about to meet Jimmy's friends and maybe even his family. She couldn't even fasten a necklace or fix a fancy hairdo with one hand.

Was that what bothered her? Did she care what his people thought?

"No, I do not. I am Jodie Cahill. I ride bulls and am a

rancher. People's opinions don't mean jack squat to me." She said the words aloud and with conviction. Her heart didn't believe them.

Her stomach growled. It had been a while since they had stopped at a convenience store and bought fruit and crackers for lunch. The apple, banana, and package of cheese crackers were gone. She didn't want to see Jimmy but going out for food without asking him if he wanted something didn't make sense. He was probably hungry too.

Sure, her conscience chided, *you've grown accustomed to having him close by and you don't like it when he's not within speaking distance.*

"Shut up. I'm hungry, not infatuated or even interested." She didn't convince herself or that niggling little voice.

Jimmy unpacked everything in his suitcases and flipped open his laptop. His story was in so he would use the time to work on the novel. The final details were sliding into place and, like Jodie said, the knowledge he'd already acquired fattened the plot and made it more believable.

He'd attended the Red Meat Club dinner as Jodie's guest, had seen enough cattle that he knew the difference in Charolais, Angus, Holstein, and Herefords, and even allowed himself to attend a llama show. Thank goodness Jodie wasn't interested in raising them on her dream ranch.

She'd been quiet on the seven hour drive from Denver

to Lincoln, alternately reading and listening to country-western music. The last three days he'd looked forward to a couple of days of separation—time to work on the novel, to think. But now that he had it, his mind was blank and his fingers rested on the keys without knowing what to type.

The phone startled him when it rang at his elbow.

"Hello?" he said cautiously.

"Hey, what's going on?" Paul asked.

"How did you know my room number?"

"I called Cathy. She knows everything."

Jimmy frowned. *Not everything. Thank goodness.*

"So how did the time go in Denver? We didn't get to talk because the trailer was so small. Did you find a million little things that irk you about her? I bet she talks while she eats and has that high-pitched giggle that you hate in women."

"No."

"Talk to me then. Surely in two weeks you're over this five-year-old little-boy infatuation."

"No."

"Is she in the room?"

"No."

"Okay, what is happening?"

"Nothing so far. She gets cranky when she's hungry. She enjoys life to the fullest. In some ways she's even more remarkable than I ever hoped she would be. I think we are becoming friends."

"That's not good, Jimmy. You took on this assignment to get over her, not befriend her. You can't get on with your life without it," Paul said.

"I'm aware of that."

"Don't take that tone with me. I'm your best friend."

"Yes, you are, but if I can't explain it to myself, how am I going to tell you what's going on? I'm grouchy because I'm tired and have writer's block."

"Grouchy I can understand. Things are certainly not going the way you hoped. Writer's block? You? Come on, you could work on that novel with the San Antonio band marching through your living room and a team of scantily clad dancers all around you. I'm worried."

"Me, too. Someone is knocking on the door. I'll be home in three or four days, and we'll make time for a long visit. Get the old therapist's hat out and shine it up," Jimmy said.

"It will be ready."

He opened the door to find Jodie leaning against the jamb. She'd changed into the pink jogging suit under the black leather coat she'd bought from the vendor in Denver. Her hair flowed naturally down past her shoulders and she didn't have on a bit of makeup. He was reminded of the times in the middle of the night when he slipped through her room in the RV on his way to the bathroom and stopped long enough to drink in the sight of her sleeping. No makeup. Brown hair everywhere on the pillow.

He'd fought the desire to brush it back away from her face then. The same feeling tried to get the upper hand again now.

"I'm going to walk over to that KFC place and get some takeout for supper. You want some?" she asked.

He grabbed his own coat from a hanger. "I'll go with you. I could use the exercise."

"All of half a block. I can bring it back," she said.

He followed her into the hallway. "I've got writer's block."

She pushed the button for the elevator to take them to the ground floor. "Does it happen often?"

"Never has before."

"What caused it?"

"Probably all the stories I've been submitting. My characters are taking a back seat to real live bull riders and . . ." He didn't finish the sentence.

She didn't push it. "I don't want to eat in the restaurant. I'd like to sit on the floor and pig out in front of the television."

"Then we'll do it in your room," he said.

"Of course. We couldn't eat in your room. Mr. Prim and Proper couldn't have food crumbs on his floor. His feet might rot off if he stepped on a bread crumb in the middle of the night."

"Are you picking a fight?"

"I'm stating a fact," she smarted off.

"Good, then it's decided. We'll eat in your room."

They ordered a meal deal so there would be extra for snacks after the rodeo that night and carried it back to the hotel.

There was something on her mind, he was sure, but he didn't want to push the point.

There was something on his mind, she was sure, but she figured he'd speak up if he wanted to share.

He flipped through channels. "Looks like there's a 'Golden Girls' marathon on television."

She carried the cardboard container to the spot in front of the television. With a flourish she opened up several napkins and spread them out on the floor. She set the food boxes in the middle and handed Jimmy a plastic fork. "We can share. Didn't think to ask for a couple of paper plates."

He opened lids to mashed potatoes, gravy, and baked beans. "So is it Blanche and Rose or do we watch something else just as mind-numbing?"

"You don't like them?"

"Yes, they are fine. I don't watch much television. Don't usually have the time."

"Oh, so you are too intellectual and your mind works on a higher plane than us mere mortals who like the 'Golden Girls'?"

"Did I say that? And you are definitely picking a fight," he said.

"Not exactly. Don't eat all the potatoes. You're working on my half."

He pushed the container toward her. "Well, excuu-use me."

She didn't know why she was so grouchy or why he couldn't do one thing to suit her but it was relieving the turmoil. She smiled.

"So KFC mashed potatoes make you smile. I should have let you have the whole order."

"Now *you* are picking a fight," she said.

"Want to start all over?" he asked.

"No, I'm ready to fight some more."

"Who's the referee? How do we know who wins?"

"I win. I always win."

He reached over and stole a fork full of potatoes. "Maybe not this time."

She attempted to stab him with her plastic fork but missed and stuck the chicken leg he held. "You aren't playing fair."

"So?"

"If you can cheat, I can too," she said.

He grinned.

Her heart melted and she didn't care about fighting anymore.

"So which one is your grandmother?" he asked.

"What?" She frowned, then realized his mind had gone back to the television show. "Oh, that would be Dorothy for sure," she said without hesitation, glad to be on familiar footing. Was that just flirting they'd done? Or was it really a fight? She'd have to think about it later.

"Why?"

"Granny Etta is tall and kind of rawboned. She's got short gray hair and even though she doesn't dress like Dorothy she's got that practical attitude. Which one is yours?"

"Blanche," he said.

Jodie almost choked on a bite of chicken. "She's a hussy?"

"Afraid so. She's not so promiscuous but she could put Blanche to shame for southern attitude and flashy dress. Rich as Midas and just as sassy."

"Your father's mother?"

"No, Mom's."

"What's her name?"

"Amelia Fleming. Ever heard of her?"

"No. Why'd you ask? Is she into the rodeo scene?"

He spewed sweet tea all over the front of his white shirt. "Good Lord, no!"

"Evidently that was the wrong question to ask."

"Not the wrong question, but the visual of her in boots and jeans is crazy. She's the CEO of a holding corporation my grandfather built before he died a few years ago. My mother works in the company with her. She's an only child so the company will be hers some-day."

"And yours?" Jodie asked.

"Not mine. I don't want an office job with nothing

but a view of downtown San Antonio. Cathy can have it if she wants it," Jimmy said.

"Cathy?"

"It's a long story."

Using the remote she turned off the television. "I've got time."

"Okay. Cathy is my stepsister. She's five years older than me. I was six and she was eleven when our parents married."

"That's all?" she asked when he stopped and didn't start again.

He nodded.

She wanted to slap more out of him. For the first time he was opening up and then the door slammed. In that moment she wanted to know more about him. What was it that drove him? What had he been like as a child? Where was his father? But she couldn't pry, not when it was evident he'd told her more than he intended to in the first place.

"Cathy has mothered me even more than my mother ever since she came into our family. When my mother and her father divorced she was eighteen and in college. By the time she finished her education there was a place for her in the corporation. She's smart and . . ."

She waited.

"Cathy is . . . I don't know how to explain it."

Jodie's ears perked right up. What was it about Cathy?

Was he in love with her even though she was so much older than him?

Jodie's heart plummeted toward the hotel basement. "You don't have to."

Better to not know than know and suffer the pain.

"Now that I've gotten started, maybe I'd better," he said. "You'll meet Cathy and you'll love her because you'll see past the problem."

Now Jodie was definitely all ears. "Thank you for that vote of confidence."

"Cathy was in a car wreck and is confined to a wheelchair. She's very opinionated and defensive because of the chair, I think. She wasn't so much that way when I was young."

"That's all? Good grief, I was expecting you to tell me she was spawned by aliens and looks like E.T.," Jodie said.

He smiled and his dimples deepened.

"So is she going to have a problem with me being six feet tall and not in a wheelchair?"

"No one would have a problem with you except when you are hungry or cranky," he said.

"Then I'll do my best to be full and on my best behavior when I meet these people. Your grandmother might intimidate me, though."

"Bulls don't intimidate you so I don't think my grandmother will," he chuckled.

Chapter Six

Jodie opened the drapes and looked out over the estate. If riches impressed her, she'd have blinking stars in her eyes. She appreciated the lovely bedroom suite, the home, even the fact that a paid staff member had carried her luggage up the winding staircase. But, and there always seemed to be a but these days, although she'd known Jimmy came from wealthy people, she'd never expected that he was in the Forbes set.

They'd left Nebraska early that morning and had driven thirteen hours, stopping only for gas and food to make it to San Antonio in time for him to have dinner with his family that night. Dinner, as in the evening meal which would be served at eight o'clock and they dressed for it; not supper, as in the evening meal served at six o'clock and everyone showed up with clean hands and hopefully no bull manure on their boots.

A four-poster king-sized bed barely took a dent out of the room. A matching chest of drawers and three-mirrored dresser held empty drawers so she could un-pack. A seating group upholstered in burgundy and ecru tapestry matched the duvet cover and pillows tossed every which way on the bed. Amongst all the finery, she felt like the only chicken at a coyote convention.

"Bluff," she mumbled. Suddenly she knew how her sister Roseanna felt amongst the rich and shameless when she first met Trey.

She ran water in an oversized tub in a bathroom bigger than her bedroom on Cahill Ranch, but she was too nervous to enjoy it. She'd allowed half an hour to laze in the tub with her cast hanging out the side, but after ten minutes she was pacing the floor wearing a towel and a frown.

She'd dressed by seven o'clock and flipped through the channels on the television, stopping at an old rerun of 'The Golden Girls.' She studied Blanche's movements and southern accent. Surely his grandmother didn't really act like that. At seven-thirty he rapped gently on her door.

"I'm ready," she said when she opened it.

She was used to seeing him in dress slacks and silk shirts, but that night he wore a three-piece black suit with a deep green shirt and matching tie. In that get-up she could see where other women might think he really was handsome.

He raised an eyebrow. "Wow! Where have you been hiding that?"

"In the bottom of my boot bag," she said but his expression renewed her flagging confidence.

She looked like she'd just stepped off a Paris runway in the simple, ankle-length black dress with a slit up the side. High-heeled shoes set her at eye level with him but with her natural cool self-assurance he didn't doubt that if she'd been six inches taller than his six feet, three inches that it would have bothered her. A diamond sparkled on the end of a silver chain ending right in the middle of her bosom. Her hair was slicked back with a silver clasp at the nape of her long, slender neck. Jimmy's mouth went as dry as if he'd just walked across the Sahara without a drop of water.

"I hope I didn't overdo it and I sure hope this is the last time we have to do this dress-for-dinner thing because this is the only fancy dress I brought with me," she said.

He looped her arm through his and led her down the hallway to the top of the stairs. "San Antonio has shops."

Three women waited at the bottom, eyeing them the whole way down. She read amusement in the older woman's eyes, amazement in the middle-aged woman's face and pure anger in the brunet in the wheelchair. Tomorrow, bright and early, she was making Jimmy take her to a hotel. A good cheap one where she could eat KFC for supper in her pink jogging suit.

Jimmy made introductions. "I want to introduce you all to Jodie Cahill, my partner in the rodeo circuit. Jodie, this is my grandmother, Amelia Fleming."

She removed her hand from his arm and offered it. "It's a pleasure."

The woman wore a multicolored sequined top over a flowing black skirt. Her gray hair was feathered back from her face in a stylish cut. The light from the chandelier caught the gleam of rubies at her neck and earlobes. She had a firm no-nonsense handshake, and Jodie could envision her in a black power suit ordering people around.

"Welcome to our home. I hope you enjoy your time here. Jimmy will have to show you the stables. Do you ride?"

Jimmy laughed. "Yes, Grandmother, she rides."

"I mean, other than bulls?" she asked.

"Yes, ma'am, and I'd love to ride while I'm here. Maybe tomorrow I could help exercise the horses."

"Feel free to do so."

Jimmy took a step. "And my mother, Lorraine Dexter."

She followed the same protocol. "I'm so glad to meet you."

Lorraine was dressed in a navy blue dress with billowing sleeves that matched her deep blue eyes. Her blond hair was done up in a french twist. She looked more like his older sister than his mother, and there was something vaguely familiar about the woman. Maybe she'd seen her face on the front of a magazine at some time, but she would swear that she'd met her before.

"As am I," Lorraine said.

One more step.

"And this is my sister, Cathy Dexter," Jimmy said.

Jodie reached out her hand and looked down into brown eyes that tried to cut her in half. "I've heard so much about you, Cathy, and it's all been good."

She wore a black jacket with velvet lapels over a lemon-colored silk blouse cut into a deep V at the neckline. It was plain to see that she hadn't been a tall woman before the accident but a confident, lovely one who would not like to be confined to a wheelchair.

"Of course it's all been good. I'm his right arm," she said.

She avoided Jodie's eyes and looked up into Jimmy's instead. Softness replaced anger as Jimmy bent to kiss her on the forehead.

"Deanna and her father as well as Ernest will be joining us," Amelia said.

Jodie looked at Jimmy who shrugged.

"Oh, stop it," Cathy said. "You know Deanna has been in love with you for more than a year."

"Stop what?"

"Acting as if you don't care," Cathy said.

"Children," Amelia smiled. "We have a guest so there won't be any bickering."

The staff member who'd carried Jodie's bags to her room appeared at the door with three people in tow. A gray-haired man in a suit, another fellow with dark hair dressed almost identically. And a beautiful, petite blond dressed in powder blue velvet, her freshly styled hair flowing down her back and her eyes on no one except Jimmy.

"James, darlin', I hoped you'd be back from the wilds tonight. This is lovely." She grabbed his hands and tip-toed for a kiss on the cheek, which he dutifully delivered.

Introductions were made. The gray-haired man was Ernest Perrin, who was Amelia's close friend and escort to social functions. The dark-haired one was Joseph Radford, Deanna's father and a friend of the family as well. Both men were visibly taken with Jodie, even with her broken arm. Deanna sized her up and down like Cathy had done earlier, as if she had ketchup on her cheeks and dirt on her chin.

"Shall we go in to dinner?" Amelia took Ernest's arm and led the way into the dining room. She allowed him to seat her at the head of the table with him to her right and Joseph to her left. Lorraine sat next to Joseph. Deanna and Jimmy sat side by side across the table from them. A chair had been removed from the place beside Jimmy for Cathy's wheelchair.

Lorraine motioned for Jodie. "Here, you are to sit beside me."

Jodie eyed the centerpiece of fresh cut flowers. She was almost hungry enough to nibble on the bright yellow marigolds and the white roses did look right appetizing. She looked across at Cathy who was busy trying to kill her appetite with go-to-the-devil looks. The woman didn't know nothing ruined Jodie's appetite. Not love. Lack of love. Witchy women. She could nibble on a hamburger while pulling a calf or eat a steak five minutes after breaking up with a feller. Cathy did have a lot to learn in the next few days.

She glanced down the table at Jimmy, who was listening intently to something Deanna was whispering. Votive candles flickering at precisely six inches apart down the length of the table kept the room dim and gave Deanna a further advantage. In the low lights she looked even more beautiful in her fancy blue velvet gown. Jodie felt like a little servant girl from the streets in one of those big old English romance novels. Too bad Jimmy wasn't darkhaired and muscular as the men who graced the front of the books. She might push back her chair, rip one shoulder out of her all-purpose black dress, and crawl down the table—blowing out the candles along the way—just to plant a big old sloppy, passionate kiss on him. Now wouldn't that just bring dinner to a screeching halt!

"And I understand you are a bull rider?" Cathy said coolly.

"That's right," Jodie answered.

Deanna shivered. "Surely you don't get on those horrible beasts and ride them."

"Yes, ma'am, I surely do."

Ernest smiled, showing off a whole mouth full of shiny dentures. "I can't understand women who do things like that, can you, Amelia?"

"Why, Ernest that's sexist. I run a corporation and I'm a woman."

"Yes, and you do it so well. But some things should be for men only. Riding bulls is too dangerous for men. Women shouldn't think of such things."

Cathy gave Jodie a knowing smile. "I agree with Ernest. It's so bohemian."

Four waiters dressed in white shirts and dark trousers moved unobtrusively delivering bowls of steaming hot lobster bisque. Jodie waited to see what Amelia would do. When she didn't ask anyone to say grace but picked up her spoon and began to eat, Jodie did the same. The waiters poured wine from a chilled bottle of Chardonnay, the buttery richness complementing the creamy bisque to perfection.

"So do you like lobster bisque?" Cathy asked.

"Love it. Granny Etta's secret for a spicier version is a splash of steak sauce. Sometimes we serve shooters at the lodge. Cool it slightly, pour it up in shot glasses, and add a dollop of crème fraîche. It's wonderful in the summertime like that. Wintertime we usually eat it hot."

Jimmy bit his lip to keep from smiling. They were baiting Jodie. It wasn't the first time he'd brought a woman home only to find it was the last time she'd go out with him. Not that he and Jodie were dating or even that it could ever be a possibility, but it was fun to see Cathy meet her match. His grandmother had deliberately seated him beside Deanna, and yes a marriage in that area would unite two very large companies. But if they wanted a merger they needed to talk to his mother and Joseph. He was not attracted to Deanna in the least bit. Short whimpering blonds were for the covers of Jodie's romance books, not his heart.

Jodie was still famished when she finished the half cup of soup and wished for more. It wasn't as good as Granny Etta's but it was filling. She would probably be sent to the gallows if she asked for a second helping. She'd have to spend the night scrubbing the toilets with a toothbrush for committing such a faux pas. She'd dang sure ask and devour a dozen bowls if she could use Jimmy's toothbrush. Sitting over there with that bit of fluff and acting as if Jodie weren't even in the room. She should have worn her jeans, the ones that needed washing, and her boots, the ones with manure on them.

When the madam at the head of the table finished, she did a little flitter of the fingers and the waiters whisked away the empty bowls and in seconds replaced them with Caesar salads. Romaine lettuce, croutons and parmesan cheese tossed with just the right amount of homemade dressing.

"Not white. I told Mohin I wanted the red wine from the Cotes. Paul Jaboulet's Parellele 45. I've found it to be a light-bodied, earthy red wine with a little spice and forward fruit flavor. Don't you think it goes better with Caesar salad than the white, Ernest?"

"Yes, it does. We talked about this last week when we had dinner at my home. You've made a wise choice. Not to say that the white wouldn't have been well received. It most certainly does complement a Caesar very well. It's just that the Parellele has a little more body and goes that extra mile."

Jodie contemplated picking up the wrong fork just to see if Cathy would jump up out of her wheelchair and do a dance on the tabletop but she used her best manners and didn't succumb to her better judgment. Not once did she cram her mouth full of salad and talk while she chewed. She kept a hand in her lap and wadded her napkin into a lump, wishing the whole time it was Jimmy's blond curls she had her fingers tied up in. Had she known this was what she was letting herself in for, she wouldn't have consented to come here even for one night. But then had she not, he would have won that little argument about her not fitting into his world any better than he did in hers. No, she'd stick it out a little longer just to show him she was the winner.

Amelia signaled the waiters, and they took away the

salad plates and half-filled wine glasses and brought on the main entrée. Sliced white turkey breast on a bed of rice with three stalks of asparagus on the side. It looked scrumptious: not Granny Etta's turkey and cornbread dressing, but Jodie could have eaten half a steer by then. Shoot the critter, lop off its horns, slap it on the grill for five minutes on each side, and serve it up with fried potatoes and okra.

Waiters poured wine from a bottle that had a brass monkey wrapped around it.

"So what do you think of our chef's stuffed nanking brined turkey with five treasure sweet rice? Doesn't the Affentaler Baden Spatburgunder go well with it?" Cathy asked.

Jodie knew she was expected to fail the test miserably. Surely a bull rider had absolutely no taste for the finer things of life. Cathy looked at her like she could see bologna sandwiches and soda pop.

The corners of Jodie's mouth turned up slightly in a sticky sweet grin. "My compliments to your chef. The wine is lovely. I enjoy a Pinot Noir with turkey. Don't you love the apple smoked bacon flavor? It's as light as a Beaujolais but has a satisfying acidity. Does your chef give out recipes? I'd love to take this one home to Granny Etta."

Cathy gave her a condescending smile. "Of course not. That's why Mohin works for us and not a lodge."

"I see," Jodie said. Come morning, she'd be gone so

fast the door wouldn't hit her in the heinie when she ran away from this place like a turpentined cat.

"Cathy, I think I hear you being snide down there," Jimmy said.

"*Moi*? Surely you jest. I was just telling the bull rider that Mohin does not give out recipes. I guess she doesn't understand the ways of a personal chef."

Jimmy ever so slyly winked at Jodie and turned his attention back to Deanna. He had no doubt Jodie could hold her own even against the present odds.

The next course was a tray of assorted fine cheese cubes and fresh fruit set before each person. Jodie read the label on the wine, a Zinfandel called Terra d'Oro from California. By that time she was barely sipping the wine.

"You don't like Grandmother's selection of wine for the fruit?" Cathy asked.

Lord, help me not to strangle this woman, Jodie prayed. *Every bite I've taken she's watched me like a hawk. She barely picks at her food but downs the wine and holds up her glass for refills. By the time this dinner is over, I'll still be hungry and she'll be an obnoxious drunk.*

"It's wonderful. However did you find such sweet strawberries and watermelon at this time of year?" Jodie asked.

"Mohin raises our vegetables and fruit in his own hydroponic garden year-round. It's amazing. Maybe tomorrow you'd like a tour so you can take ideas home for your little lodge?"

"No, thank you. I'm always glad to see the garden die out in the winter. Can't wait for the first green beans and new potatoes but by the time fall arrives, I'm sick of picking beans."

Deanna was visibly aghast. "You surely don't do it yourself?"

"Yes, ma'am, I surely do. On the ranch we aren't exempt from work just because we are women. I drive a tractor, bale hay, clean out horse stalls, and pick beans. It's all in a day's work." Jodie's voice was silky smooth.

But Jimmy heard the edge.

"Admirable," Joseph said. "And your father, what does he do?"

"The same thing."

"I see. Why are you traveling with James? Surely you aren't riding bulls with a broken arm?"

"No, if it weren't for the broken bone I would be, though. There's a lot of money at stake and someday I hope to buy my own ranch," she said.

"And run it by yourself?" Deanna asked.

"That's right."

"You are a brave woman. Kind of like those pioneers in the history books we used to read about, huh, Cathy?"

"That's not brave. That's foolhardy. I saw a cartoon once where one old dirt farmer said to the other, 'I'd give you a million dollars but you'd just ranch it all up.'

The market is going toward the bigger production companies. Little Oklahoma ranches don't stand a chance in the futuristic scheme of things."

Jodie pushed the wine back. "I disagree. If a person is wanting to make a million dollars a year or even half a million, then they'd best stay away from ranching. But there is still a good honest living to be had off the land, and it's a wonderful way to raise children."

"What do you think, James?" Deanna asked.

"I have to agree with Jodie. She'll be a good rancher. She knows the business and studies the markets. Her children will grow up to be as stable and responsible as she is."

Deanna shuddered again. "To each his own. My children will grow up in the corporate world and all it can offer them and will be just as stable and responsible."

Amelia patted her hand. "Yes, they certainly will. And you'll make a wonderful mother."

Jimmy felt the icy glare his grandmother shot him. The lines had been drawn and the war declared. What was it they saw in Jodie Cahill that made them close ranks and pull out the big cannons? She threatened them to the extent that they were pushing Deanna at him at a fast pace. If they knew the way he felt about Jodie they'd probably put arsenic in her after-dinner coffee. Thank goodness, he'd never mentioned her to anyone but Paul and Paul was sworn to secrecy.

Dessert was served with a lovely white wine which

Jodie completely ignored. The tiramisu was comparable to what was served at the Spaghetti Warehouse in Oklahoma City. Greta would salivate over it as much or more than that Mustang parked in the Cahill Ranch garage. Jodie remembered her telling about eating it when she and Kyle chaperoned the youth group from the church a few weeks ago.

Amelia and Ernest talked shop: This company was about to merge with that one and they would need to sell stock in another. Deanna kept whispering to Jimmy but kept an eye on Jodie in her peripheral vision. Cathy made no bones about it, she glared at Jodie. Joseph and Lorraine spoke in low tones about a Valentine's Day dance at the club and whether or not James would be back to escort Deanna.

Jodie was the only one at the table who'd eaten all of her dessert and left the wine untouched. She was ready to leave at that moment but her grandmother would have her hide if she wasn't polite, even in present company.

"Please bring coffee to the library," Amelia told a waiter.

Thank goodness, this evening is over. Tomorrow I'm out of here. I don't care if Jimmy does think he's won and that I can't handle his lifestyle. Truth is, I can't. I'm still hungry and aggravated to boot.

Ernest looped Amelia's arm through his. Joseph did the same with Lorraine. And Deanna grabbed Jimmy's hand. That left Cathy and Jodie.

Cathy glared. Jodie glowered right back.

"If you will excuse me, I'm very tired. I think I'll skip coffee and go straight up to my room," Jodie said as they left the dining room.

"Yes, of course," Amelia said.

Cathy smirked. She'd won.

Deanna looked relieved, and Lorraine and Joseph barely noticed her absence.

It took a good portion of her willpower to keep from slamming the door so hard it rattled the pictures from the landing walls. She kicked off her shoes, removed the clasp at the back of her neck and slung the necklace down on the dresser, undressed as fast as she could with one arm, and started hot water running in the shower. She needed to wash away the feeling those people had evoked. She wrapped her arm in a grocery bag, secured the top with a rubber band, and stepped into the steaming stall.

Why did you let them provoke you? You've not played your cards so well, my granddaughter. Etta's voice was as clear as if she were propped up on the vanity. *You must like that James Crowe or this wouldn't matter. Remember how you used to come home from Tulsa in a snit because Rosy loved Trey so much she let people aggravate her? You are doing the same thing.*

"It's not true. He's not my type and he's always going to be a prissy rich boy, and I'm not going to like him. And if I do start liking him, then I will stop."

She toweled herself dry after fifteen minutes, put on her most ragged old sleep shirt, and curled up in front of the television to watch another episode of 'The Golden Girls.'

"Amelia isn't Blanche. Even with her sass and brassiness, Blanche has got more feelings that that woman," she mumbled.

The rerun couldn't hold her attention so she went to the window and looked out over the estate at night. Apparently the party had ended, because Lorraine was walking with Joseph out to his car. He kissed her lightly on the cheek. A lover's kiss? A friend's peck? Who knew and who cared?

Amelia's white hair glistened in the moonlight. Ernest said something and she touched his shoulder, the two of them looking a long time at each other. There was no kiss or hug, just a friendly wave.

Jodie was about to turn back to see what Sophia was saying to make everyone on the TV laugh when Jimmy and Deanna strolled out to a fancy little sports car parked beside Jodie's truck. Deanna wrapped her arms around his neck and, on tiptoe, pulled his face down to hers for a long, lingering kiss. She didn't want to watch but she couldn't take her eyes from the sight. So Deanna and Jimmy had something going between them and Jodie was just jealous bait. She couldn't get out of this place fast enough. It would be a hard decision not to call the CEO and tell him to cancel the rest of her judging.

You going to let her win? Granny Etta's voice asked.

"No, but I sure want to right now," Jodie said aloud.

Jimmy knew what Jodie meant that night when she said Chris's kiss was boring. Deanna was good at what she did, but it bored him. He'd rather have had Jodie standing toe to toe, eye to eye with him, fighting and then making up. He was alive when she was around. Not just going through the motions, but heart thumping, bantering living. He would have far rather been sitting on the floor in a hotel room stealing mashed potatoes than eating a five-course meal and drinking good wine.

It had backfired. This idea that he could get her out of his mind if he spent time with her. He'd just have to work harder. He still had two months to take care of it. Maybe by then he wouldn't have the desire to wipe Deanna's kisses off his mouth.

Chapter Seven

Jodie was loaded for bear the next morning. Expecting a forty-course meal with waiters and the whole nine yards, she was surprised when she there was no one in the dining room but Jimmy. His gray jogging suit was damp with sweat and his blond curls were limp.

"Good morning. I've already had a run and breakfast. What would you like? I'll have the chef prepare it," he said.

She sat down at the end of the table, far away from him. "I'd like a taxi, a hotel room, and a lot less witchy women."

"That was a little overdone last night, wasn't it?"

"If it had been a steak, it wouldn't have been a little overdone, it would have been charred black. I don't intend to stay a whole week in this house and live with that kind of treatment."

"I'm sorry, I truly am, but last night won't happen again," he said.

"You can guarantee such a thing?"

"Yes, I can. Tonight we are having dinner with Paul. I told you I'd introduce you to him. After that we'll be at the rodeo every night doing our jobs. During the day, they are all downtown at the office. By the time they get home in the evening, we'll be gone and when we come in they'll be in bed. You probably won't see any of them again. And by the way, that was standard procedure last night. Every woman I've ever brought home got that kind of treatment. That's why there's no one in my life. Haven't found one who'll stick around once they figure out they've got those three to deal with."

"Deanna does."

"Deanna is different. Grandmother has her picked out to be my wife. Mother thinks it's a wonderful idea, and Cathy would be happy with the arrangement because it would merge two big companies together."

"And you?"

"Me? I don't love her and I've got this old-fashioned notion that people marry each other for love, not for business. Now what would you like for breakfast?"

"Bacon, eggs, biscuits, gravy, and hot coffee."

"That's what I figured. I already told the chef. It'll be ready in five minutes. Want to glance at the morning paper? Your name is in it as one of the judges for the rodeo's bull riding. You figure you'll ever get back on a bull?"

"Probably." He'd just said he didn't love Deanna so was he leading her on by whispering through dinner with her and then kissing her? It was on the tip of her tongue to ask in a not-so-nice tone when she realized she didn't want the answer.

"How about you, Jodie? Why aren't you married?"

"Because I haven't found someone I can live with," she said honestly.

"You mean someone you can't live without?"

"No, I meant what I said. Living without means falling madly in love and that's all right but it's not the be-all, end-all. If you can't live with a person, it doesn't matter if you love them or not. Reckon that chef has my breakfast ready?"

"He'll send it out when he does," Jimmy said. So she had ideas of her own about what a relationship should entail and she'd put it so well. He'd been in love with her or the image he'd created of her since he was five years old. However, living and loving were indeed two different things. He was pretty dang sure he could never live with a bull riding, ranching woman.

A staff member brought her breakfast on a tray and set it before her.

"Thank you so much. This looks delicious," she said.

He nodded and went back to the kitchen.

"What would you like to do today? The Alamo, River-walk, shopping?"

"Shop," she said.

"That was easy. Anything in particular you want to look for?"

"Just take me to a mall and you can even sit outside and read a book or take notes for your novel. I just need a few things," she said. She wasn't going to wear her one black dress again that night.

"Then I will go shower and get ready for an afternoon in a mall. Oh, tonight's dinner is informal. Paul is barbecuing in his backyard since we've got a couple of days of decent weather. We'll be eating buffet style in his dining room with two other couples."

"Jeans?" She raised an eyebrow.

"Should be fine. I'll go on up and get a shower," he said.

No, it wouldn't. She wouldn't overdress but she wasn't going to underplay the casual idea either. She'd already felt like a country bumpkin in the White House and it had not been pleasant.

The waiter brought a telephone to the table and handed it to her. "For you, Miss Jodie."

"Thank you," she smiled. "Hello," she said expecting to hear her Granny Etta's voice on the other end.

"Oh, you're still there," Cathy said smoothly. "I hope your room was satisfactory and you slept well."

"Very well," Jodie answered.

"I suppose you are wondering why I'm calling?"

"Yes, ma'am."

"I am arranging a room at the Ramada for you. I think you will be comfortable there for the rest of the week. A taxi will arrive in an hour. That should be enough time to get your things ready."

"Why?"

"Because you aren't going to live in the same house with James for a whole week."

"Why? We lived together in an RV that wasn't nearly as big as my bedroom here. And you set up the arrangements so you already know that. We are colleagues, not lovers, Cathy."

"Don't give me that line. I figured you were some big, overweight woman who didn't know she was a female but I was wrong. I can see the way he looks at you and it would never work. I've done my homework. You are just a rancher's daughter. James has been groomed for something bigger and better than that. His mother took him out of that scenario when he was five years old and she'd die if he went back to it. Your taxi will be there shortly. You need to be packing."

Jodie sucked in a lung full of air. "Sorry, doll. I'm here at Jimmy's invitation. I'll do my best to stay out of your way, believe me, but you're not running me off. If Jimmy wants me gone, he'll tell me. Now you have a nice day, honey, and don't you be worrying your little head about me stealing away the family jewel."

"Don't you get snippy with me. You aren't wanted. Go away. He has to work with you because he needs you for the articles. Don't be thinking you'll worm your way into his heart and fortune. I'll make sure that doesn't happen no matter what it takes," Cathy said icily.

"Money has never impressed me and if I wanted Jimmy's love, nobody would keep me from having it. I'm not easily scared, Cathy. Good-bye, now." Jodie carefully pushed the button. Whew! No wonder poor old Jimmy was still single. Bless his poor baby heart.

She finished the last dregs of cold coffee and went to her room feeling much better. Maybe she just needed a healthy cat fight to clear the air. She hummed as she got dressed.

Jimmy had no idea where to take Jodie shopping. His clothing was all tailored and he never frequented malls. He started to call Cathy to ask her advice but after the way she'd baited Jodie at dinner the night before, he hesitated. Finally he dialed Paul's home number and asked Sara. She suggested North Star Mall on San Pedro since they had Saks, Macy's, and Dillards, in addition to the biggest cowboy boots in the world. Standing forty-feet high and twenty-feet long, that alone was a tourist attraction. Besides, Jodie was a rodeo girl and she'd appreciate the sight.

She opened the door to her room at the same time he started out of his at the end of the hallway. She wore jeans, boots, a blouse with flowing sleeves to accommodate the cast, and her big black leather overcoat. She'd left her hair down, and he had the strangest desire to run his fingers through it to see if it was really as soft as it looked.

She tossed him the keys to the truck. "I'm ready."

He promptly threw them back. "My turf. My car. I'll drive."

She cocked her head to one side. "Yes, sir!"

He smiled. His dimples deepened. She reined in her racing heart.

She half expected him to tell her to fold her long, lanky legs up in the vintage Corvette sitting in the six car garage but he bypassed that one and opened the door to a 1958 Ford Thunderbird: red with white leather interior. She bit the inside of her lip to keep from grinning like a sophomore out on her first date. Now, this was a car she might drool on; no doubt Greta would be speechless.

"Nice car," she said.

"I like it. It was my grandfather's car. He bought it brand spanking new right off the showroom floor in 1958. He passed it on to me when I turned sixteen."

"Along with the 'vette and the Mustang?" she asked.

"No, those two I bought myself," he answered. "But my grandfather loved old cars and we talked about them often before he died."

"I'm sorry," she said.

"Thank you."

He parked at the shopping mall entrance beside the tall boots. Jodie was amazed with them.

"You've got to take a picture of me with these. Here, use my cell phone and I'll send it over the 'net to my sister. I can't wait for her husband to see this picture. He wears a size fourteen and we tease him all the time about having a very good understanding," she said.

"That would be Trey?"

"No, Trey wouldn't be caught dead in cowboy boots. It's Matt, Vicky's husband. Trey is the black sheep. He doesn't rodeo or ranch, either. I wondered what on earth Rosy saw in him, but she must love him. She's married him twice."

He snapped three pictures, hoping the light was good enough that he'd get one good one. He would've bought the boots for her if they'd been for sale. Suddenly, he drew himself up short. This whole excursion was to get her out of his system. It was certainly not to write her name there in indelible ink.

He handed the phone back. "So why did Roseanna marry Trey twice?"

"They fell in love, got married in Vegas the first time, and both of them were miserable. He comes from the same kind of folks you do. Rich enough to buy Fort Knox out of petty cash and flamboyant with it."

He held up a hand. "Hey, wait a minute. We are very, very comfortable but we couldn't buy Fort Knox and we are not flamboyant."

She cut her eyes around at him. "You better open your eyes, James Moses. What would you call that dinner last night if not flamboyant?"

"It's a simple dinner party among friends. Grandmother does one about once a week and attends two or three each week at other friends' homes. She is very social."

"Honey, if that was simple, I don't want to see anything extravagant," she said. "And while I'm thinking about it, what did Cathy mean when she said your mother got you out of a scenario like ranching when you were five years old?"

Jimmy's mind went into overdrive. What to say? What not to say without giving the whole thing away? "My father is . . . he was . . ." Jimmy stammered.

"Alive or dead?" She sat down on a bench.

"Dead," he said.

"Then it's *'my father was'* and I'm sorry about that too. If you don't want to tell me, it's all right. I was prying and that's not fair," she said.

"My father was a ne'er-do-well. He was my grandfather's driver and mechanic. Mother was going through what Grandmother calls a rebellious time in her life. Eighteen. Out of high school. About to go to college. They fell in love and eloped. Grandfather offered him money to go away. He turned him down, and they went to California where he tried to get into acting. Then it was Las Vegas where he was a blackjack dealer and that's where I was born. Then Texas where he worked on an oil rig and, well, we moved an awful lot. Anyway, one day he died in a horse accident. From what I can understand he was riding a horse down into a gully to round up some cattle at a ranch where he worked. The horse slipped, reared, and rolled. My father couldn't get out of the saddle and the horse crushed him. Mother called Grandfather. He brought me and Mother home. We had lived on that ranch about six weeks. Mother hated it worse than the Texas oil rig town and Las Vegas. I guess that's what Cathy was referring to."

"Okay, let's go shopping. I want a new outfit to wear tonight, and you have to help me," she changed the subject even though her curiosity was not satisfied.

"Oh, no. You said I could sit on the bench and read a book," he protested.

"I lied," she said.

"But . . ."

"If you can lie, I can too."

He threw up his hands. "I didn't lie."

"No, you just sugarcoated the truth and didn't tell the whole story. I just lied but I can sugarcoat it now. You've sat on the bench and you can read the tags on whatever I try on and tell me how much it costs."

"What makes you say I sugarcoated the truth, and why is it okay for you to do it and not me?" His dimples weren't showing. His voice had the same edge she'd heard when they argued over taking his fancy little Mustang on a road trip.

"I talked you into going shopping, didn't I?"

"I will get even," he declared.

"I'll look forward to seeing you try," she said.

"I'll make a deal with you. I'll go into Dillards, and if you don't find anything then you're on your own," he said.

She stuck out her hand. "Deal."

He thought he was getting off easy until he took her hand. The shock about blew him out of his shoes. He wanted to drag her closer, push her hair back from that vulnerable place on her neck and begin kissing her there, move up to her eyelids and then down to those full lips. If only a handshake could cause that reaction, he wondered how he was ever going to get her out of his mind.

The heat from his touch warmed her heart and melted her soul. A simple contact with his fingers had set her to thinking about a long kiss that would not be boring. It was time to go home and forget about modeling clothing for this man but she couldn't think of a single way to get out of it gracefully. She'd conned the fiddler into playing and now it was time to pay, but oh my, the price was so high.

She chose three outfits from a rack and took them to the dressing room. Her hands shook as she tried on a dress with a spliced, overlapping bodice and a full skirt.

The sleeves flowed down from the elbow so the cast wasn't a problem but the top exposed more cleavage than she wanted him to see. However, if he had to sit outside then she was obligated to model. She tugged at the dark green challis in an attempt to cover more of her chest and raised her chin. He would not know how much he'd affected her by merely grasping her hand.

Jimmy sat on one of three chairs just outside and waited. Actually the chair was more comfortable than the benches in the mall's center court and he was proving a point. No woman could find an outfit by shopping in a single store. After this she'd be on her own for the rest of the day, and he'd send someone to pick her up. He didn't care if she did think he and his family were flamboyant.

When she walked out of the dressing room, his mouth literally went dry. In an effort at lightheartedness she twirled around. Through a photographer's eye he caught at least a dozen pictures for a model's portfolio.

"So? Will this do for Paul's party?"

"Very well," he said. "Buy it and let's go."

"Oh, you don't get off that easy. There are two more in there," she said with a giggle a notch too high-pitched.

She tried on a long denim skirt with a side zipper and a bulky ecru-colored fisherman's sweater.

He would have loved to have a camera and her wearing that outfit on a pier with dark clouds rolling across the sky in the background. He could see the picture done in black and white: matted and framed in something antique, maybe oval.

The third outfit was a bright red wool straight skirt and black silk blouse with wide cuffs fastened with red buttons.

He envisioned her propped up on a stool in front of a black background. Touch her lips with a hint of red lipstick and it would be a breathtaking modern photo.

"Now what do you think?" she asked.

"For the barbecue, the white sweater and denim skirt. But you should buy all of it, Jodie. They are all very becoming and you can use the other two for church."

"And that, darlin', would be flamboyant! I'll respect your judgment and buy the denim outfit because you know your friends and what they'll be wearing." She reached out and tweaked the dimple on his left cheek. When she got back to the dressing room, her fingers were still warm.

Chapter Eight

One of the other women patted the empty barstool when Sara led Jodie into the oversized country kitchen. "Come over here and sit by me. I saw you ride five years ago. It was on television and I have to admit I wasn't a bit interested but my husband was watching it. When you got on that bull I was glued to the TV. Honey, I think I held my breath for the full eight seconds and I cheered when you got the buckle."

"Thank you," Jodie said.

"That would be Marsha and the other one is Kerstin," Sara said. She arranged pre-cut vegetables on a big blue plastic divided tray that already had a white dip in the center.

"We don't stand much on formality around here,"

124

Kerstin said. "Our husbands have all been friends for years. Went to the same school together. So did Sara. Marsha and I are the outsiders but we're learning to fit in with them."

"So, is your husband a writer also?" Jodie asked.

"No, he's a teacher, and Marsha's is still in med school."

"And I'm a nurse until he finishes and we can begin having a family," Marsha said.

"What about you, Kerstin?"

"I'm a CPA," she answered.

Sara set a glass of sweet tea in front of Jodie. "And I am finally a stay-at-home mother with two kids: Garrett, two years old, and Abigail, six months. Love staying home with them but I'm glad Mother was available to keep them tonight so we can have some adult time."

"Thanks," Jodie said and listened to them talk about their lives. It was like an audio soap opera and she knew none of the characters.

"Forgive us. We are so used to doing this once a month that we forget you don't know a thing we're talking about," Sara said.

"It's fine. If you were in Sulphur and my sister and our friends got together, it would be the same thing. Go on, please. Don't let me put a damper on the evening."

"Well, thank you. Did you hear that Deanna made the comment that if Jimmy doesn't wake up and make some kind of commitment, she's off to Italy with Bobby Jack?"

Jodie's ears perked right up.

"Her father will stroke out. Bobby Jack might be husband material for me, but not for the almighty Deanna," Sara said.

"Oh, are you still interested in Bobby Jack? I must tell Paul," Marsha smiled. One eye tooth overlapped the one beside it and freckles covered her face. The twinkle in her eye gave her an impish look that Jodie warmed right up to.

"Paul doesn't know that I ever dated that man and it was only one time. Mercy, all Bobby Jack is interested in is getting the next leg up on the corporate ladder. Come to think of it, he might be just the ticket for Deanna," Sara said. Her short red hair was styled in a spiky 'do that went well with faded jeans and a tie-dyed top.

"I heard Deanna was at Amelia's dinner party last night. Got anything to report?" Kerstin asked Jodie.

Jodie shook her head. "She seemed pretty charmed with Jimmy. Maybe Bobby Jack is just a jealous card."

"Could be," Sara said.

And they went on to other gossip which didn't interest Jodie at all. She listened with one ear and stole glances out the picture window at the men around the grill and wooden picnic table on the patio. Which one went with which woman?

"Okay, talk." Paul said when Jimmy arrived. "We've been waiting. Is it going to be a long two more months?"

"Yes, it is," Jimmy said.

"Explain."

"It's not working so well. I'm afraid it was a fool's mission. I'm finding more to like than dislike."

Paul wiped his forehead in mock horror. "Whew! Backfired, did it?"

Jimmy nodded. "So far that's the way it's going, but I've got two months to take care of it, and I will. When I come back to San Antonio, you have to buy me a steak. And you two have to set me up with a woman who can endure Amelia, Mother, and Cathy."

"There's only Superman, not Superwoman. A woman would have to have super powers for sure to endure that bunch of women," Mark, Kerstin's husband, grinned.

Jimmy smiled. "You should've seen the way Cathy baited Jodie last night and she didn't make a single point. She was worse than ever and Jodie held her own so there may be a superwoman amongst us even as we breathe and live."

Kevin set his tea glass down with a thump. "You are kidding. You found Superwoman on your own and you're going to toss her out? What's the matter with you? Mark and I are afraid to introduce you to our friends. They'd hate us after a dinner with your relatives."

Paul came to the women's defense. "Ah, they just love him too much. Don't want him to get tied up with a gold digger."

"Love. Controlling. It all adds up to smothering,"

Jimmy said. "I wish Grandfather was still alive. He kept the balance."

"Give it up and come back to San Antonio. Tell her you're tired of the travel. Tell her you are marrying Deanna. Anything. It's not going to work, man. It's going to make it harder not easier," Paul said.

"Not until I'm over the infatuation," Jimmy said. "Now how about them Spurs? Y'all think they're going to be any good news this year?"

Back on familiar ground and away from affairs of the heart, the other men all began to talk at once about sports.

The table was set with heavy stone plates in multicolors, good serviceable stainless steel flatware, tea goblets, and oversized cotton napkins. Dinner was served buffet style, right off the kitchen bar: grilled steaks big enough to fill half the plate, hash brown casserole, baked beans, cornbread, and raw vegetables with a smoky dip that Jodie intended to have the recipe for before she left that night.

"Grab a plate from the table and help yourself," Sara said.

No one had to beg Jodie. She was second in line right behind Jimmy, who wasn't showing signs of bashfulness either.

She carried her plate to the table and claimed a spot. "This smells scrumptious."

Jimmy sat right beside her. "Paul has the magic touch when it comes to steaks on the grill."

"Yes, he does," she agreed after the first bite.

"Did you tell Jodie that this is our first dinner party in our new home?" Paul asked Sara.

"No, I forgot, but I guess you just told her," Sara answered.

"My grandmother on my father's side decided to move out of this place into a condo in town. We all thought she was crazy but she swears it's the best move she ever made. She and Grandpa inherited this ranch from his father back when they were first married. She sold all of it but the five acres around the house that she gave to Sara and me and we moved in last month."

"So are you going to like living in the country?" Jodie asked. She should have known Paul before Sara snagged him. He was the tall, dark, handsome one with dark brown eyes set under heavy lashes. His arms were muscular enough to wrestle a good-sized Angus bull to the ground and she liked his smile. Just the kind of man who'd be found on the front of a romance book and who she'd always hoped for but he was branded and she didn't steal cattle or men.

"We haven't decided if we're going to like being so far away from the city but we aren't going to complain if we don't," Sara said. "It's a better place to raise the children, away from the inner urban influence. And I love this big old ramblin' house. Lord knows we could never afford anything like this, not even if I went back to nursing work."

Jimmy's arm brushed Jodie's when he reached for the salt. The contact made her suck air for a moment.

"Cornbread too hot?" Sara giggled. "Sometimes I put too many jalapeños in it."

"No, I just bit into a pepper and it took my breath." Jodie hoped she covered the gasp.

"Anyway, we moved here from a small two bedroom apartment in the city and it's been an adjustment," Paul said.

Sara pointed down a long hallway. "Four bedrooms on that end. The master suite on that end." She pointed the opposite direction. "And this great room that houses the living room-den combination, country kitchen and dining area. Thank goodness she left some furniture or there would be echoes in the house since we had so little to put in it."

Jodie wondered if Jimmy would inherit the Fleming mansion? What would his wife think of the winding staircase, the need for a domestic staff? Would she bring her own things into the marriage and toss part of Amelia's out in the yard for a garage sale?

That visual brought a smile to her face. Amelia would rise up out of her grave and come back to life if Jimmy's wife set up a garage sale in her front yard. It might just be the very thing that made Cathy walk again. She'd run out the front door and put a bullet between the new bride's eyes and Jimmy would be a grieving widower before the honeymoon was over.

"Whatever are you thinking about?" Kerstin asked.

Jodie jerked her thoughts back to the present. "I was just listening."

"Sugarcoating, are you?" Jimmy teased.

"Actually my mind was drifting and suddenly I had an image of Deanna on the back of a big black bull, one hand around the bull rope, her free hand up with diamonds sparkling and a pink cowboy hat on her head," she lied.

That brought on full-fledged laughter. Paul had to wipe his eyes with his napkin. Sara put her hand over her mouth and got the hiccups. Mark slapped Jimmy on the back and declared that he liked Jodie. Kerstin and Marsha both looked stunned.

"Now that is an impossible visual. Deanna would never wear pink. She's a powder blue girl," Kevin said.

More laughter and this time Kerstin and Marsha joined in, nodding their heads the whole time.

"I hear that she's already hired a wedding planner, and they're working on a summer wedding so she can have those new light blue roses everywhere," Paul said.

Jimmy flinched ever so slightly but Jodie saw it.

"Bobby Jack know about that?" Marsha asked.

"Bobby Jack won't care. He's got a boot on the ladder going up. If she wants to get married by an Elvis impersonator in Las Vegas, he'd be all for it. What he wants is a marriage license with no prenups, right, Jimmy?" Paul teased.

Marsha came to his rescue. "Leave Jimmy alone. He's trying to outrun the woman. He's not interested in her, are you, Jimmy?"

"What about them Spurs? You think they'll have a good season?" he asked.

"And that's that about Deanna," Mark said.

"Tell me, Jodie, how do you judge a bull riding event?" Kerstin asked.

She gave them the longest version she could think of so Jimmy would have time to digest the gossip. Maybe he really did have feelings for the woman and hadn't even realized it until confronted with another man on the scene. He'd have to sort it all out on his own, but a few minutes to regain his composure would be helpful.

"Why do they wear those vests with all that writing and advertisement on them?" Mark asked.

"Cody Lambert invented that vest. He is a former professional bull rider. It is designed to prevent injury when a rider gets stomped on or gored by a bull. It's made of Kevlar, the same material used to make bullet-proof vests. It helps protect bones and internal organs that could be vulnerable to injury if crushed by a two thousand pound bull," she explained.

Sara raised her hand like a school girl. "I've got a question. What is it that they're putting in their vest pocket right after they get off the bull?"

"His or her mouth guard."

"You mean like a football mouth guard? Why would they wear one of those?" Sara asked.

"To keep from knocking their teeth out when they fall," Jodie explained.

"So are you going to get back on a bull? I mean after you get your arm broken on one, it would be tough to get back on one, wouldn't it?" Marsha asked.

"I've been riding since I was too young to have fear and never got a broken bone. Lots of bruises, but no major problems. I didn't break my arm riding a bull. I slipped on ice out by the barn and fell. I can ride a bull. It don't mean I'm graceful," she said.

Jimmy silently disagreed. No one could be more graceful than Jodie in that black dress last night. The way she floated down the stairs beside him, her back straight, hair slicked back, she looked like she'd taken ballet lessons her whole life. Her poise and elegance couldn't have been outdone by anyone in the whole state of Texas.

"When do you get the cast off?" Kerstin asked.

"Next week. I'm friends with the rodeo doctor who'll be in Yuma at the Jaycee's Silver Spur Rodeo. He'll remove it and make sure everything is working all right. And it won't be a minute too soon. It itches something terrible."

"I broke my ankle when I was about ten," Marsha said. "Momma finally gave me a plastic fly swatter. It worked wonderful to scratch the itch. You got to have had a broken bone to know what we're talking about."

"You got that right," Jodie said.

The rest of the evening bonded her into their friendship and she was sorry when it was time to leave. They invited her to come back anytime and she promised if she decided to ride at a televised event, she'd let them know so they could watch.

"I like your friends. I really enjoyed the evening," she said.

"Good. Maybe it will make up for last night," he said.

"Oh, it wasn't so bad now that I look back. I've been in worse situations. They wouldn't be so catty if they didn't love and want to protect you from gold diggers."

"Is that what you think they thought of you?" He frowned.

She nodded.

"Why?"

"Gut feeling."

He parked the Thunderbird in the garage and they went into the house through the back door and the kitchen area. Jodie gasped when she saw the man behind the huge island in the middle of a room bigger than most restaurant kitchens. He was six feet four inches at least because he looked down on her. A rim of bright red hair circled his otherwise bald head. Crystal blue eyes glittered in a bed of wrinkles and underneath almost burgundy brows.

"Jodie, meet Mohin," Jimmy said casually.

"Mohin?" She repeated the name. The chef. He was supposed to be from the Far East and have dark skin and black eyes that matched his equally black hair which would be covered in a big white hat. Not wearing faded jeans, a tie-dyed T-shirt and cowboy boots with silver-tipped toes.

"Ah, that's a crock. My name is George and that's what you call me, lassy. George Mohindovitch. Part Polish. Part Irish. Miz Amelia likes the Mohin because it sounds all fancy. But I'm just George to my friends and you are going to be my friend. I can tell because you eat a decent breakfast."

"Thank you," Jodie smiled up at him. Well, didn't the world turn 'round. She was glad she'd stayed around and hadn't let Cathy run her off. What other miracles were ready to be discovered in the next week?

When they reached her bedroom door, Jimmy stopped. "I really did enjoy the evening. I plan on catching up on writing tomorrow but please feel free to go out to the stables and ride or explore the grounds. There're lots of staff members who'll answer questions or give you directions."

She looked up into his mossy green eyes and for a moment saw straight into his soul. She looped her free arm around his neck and leaned forward. Mouth met mouth in a kiss that did more than send tingles up her spine like his hand touching hers had done earlier that day. It dang sure wasn't boring, and she had no desire to cross her eyes during the process either like she had done with Chris. She wanted the kiss to go on forever; she wanted it to lead to more.

With a moan she stepped back and opened the door with her free hand. "I'm sorry. It was the moment."

He leaned in and kissed her on the forehead. "I'm not sorry. Good night, Jodie. I'll see you sometime tomorrow."

Chapter Nine

Jodie looked down at her castless arm. The skin looked like it needed a major scrubbing to get rid of the scales and her wrist was stiff. She'd almost panicked until the doctor assured her that three or four weeks of therapy would put the movement range back into play.

"I know these exercises look silly but they'll work. That and your everyday life. Brushing your hair. Buttoning a coat. Tying your shoes. It's all therapy. You'll be surprised by how much the muscle will return in a few weeks. Are you planning on riding this season?" the doctor asked.

She held up the hand and stared at it glumly. "No. Are you sure that this is going to work again?"

"I'm very sure."

An hour later she was dressed and in the judges' box at the Yuma Jaycee's Silver Spur Rodeo. February in Yuma was a pleasant change after Denver and Lincoln where they'd frozen in the snow drifts. The temperature was a nice seventy-five degrees and Jodie had worn a pink Western shirt with fitted sleeves, slim-fitting jeans, and her highly polished eel cowboy boots. She'd tried to sweep her hair up into a twist but the left hand refused to cooperate so it hung loose, framing her face.

Jimmy had a camera slung around his neck and a clipboard in his hands, taking notes and snapping pictures alternately. He'd left his boots at the hotel, along with the warm socks. He loved the weather. Maybe someday he'd relocate to Yuma. According to the Internet it was one of the fastest growing towns in the United States. Most likely that was due to the weather which was a wonderful change from all that snow and ice in the north. He aimed the camera at the judges' box and took another picture of Jodie. She'd been so disappointed in her wrist that afternoon. If he could've brought down a miracle from heaven he would have done so and made it perfect in an instant.

The gate opened and the first rider and bull exploded from the chute. Almost a ton of black rage tried to get rid of the man on his back. The rider slipped after three seconds and touched the bull with his free hand. In the next second the bull changed directions and the rider landed in a puff of dust. The bull fighters kept the animal occupied while the rider dusted himself off and stood to the applause of the crowd.

At the end of the evening he expected Jodie to want to go to breakfast with her friends, but she surprised him when she wanted to go back to the hotel. At midnight they were sitting in her room eating fried chicken from Wal-Mart.

"You're moody tonight," he said.

"I am not!"

"Then why aren't we in a pancake house with a bunch of people?"

"Because I didn't want pancakes. I wanted fried chicken and potato salad." She wasn't about to tell him her true feelings. The past few days have been wonderful but she had spent very little of it with him. After that kiss, she'd almost pouted when he stayed in his room most of the time. Sure, she'd gotten to know the staff. She and George exchanged recipes in the kitchen and he'd even allowed her to help him prepare her own breakfast a few times. That was quite a concession since no one touched George's kitchen. Then there were the guys out in the stables and the upstairs maid who befriended her and asked advice about a boyfriend.

And all the while the kiss was the foremost thing on her mind. How to deal with the emotions it set off? Was it really just the moment or could she possibly be falling for Jimmy—the worst choice on the face of the great green Earth?

Jodie didn't see any more of Cathy but the last day she did talk to her on the phone. Cathy coolly told her good-bye and Jodie just as coolly thanked her for her hospitality. Granny Etta would have had her hide tacked to the smokehouse door if she'd been rude, even to a catty woman like Cathy.

Jodie started humming an old Charley Pride tune, "It's Gonna Take a Little Bit Longer." Where the tune came from, she had no idea, but the words began filtering through the tune as she ate. Charley sang about it taking longer for him to ever get his woman off his mind because he'd been loving her a long, long time.

It might take a long time for Jodie to get over that kiss but she could do it. The arm would heal and so would all the emotions rattling around in her body like a marble in a tin can.

Jimmy had grown up with a grandfather who listened to country music out in the garage while he worked on his old cars. He'd had a radio on the shelf and kept it cranked up as loud as it could go. He recognized the tune the minute Jodie started humming but when he began to remember the lyrics, it was an omen from a prophet.

It was taking longer for him to get Jodie off his mind because he had been loving her a long time. When the words came to mind about wanting her more and more every day, he realized he wasn't going to get over her. It was a futile attempt and that one kiss they'd shared back in San Antonio had done nothing but prove what Charley sang in his song. Truth was he'd flat fallen in love with Jodie Cahill, the adult, even more than he'd been in love with Jodie, the five-year-old, and he didn't have any idea what to do about it.

"You sing that song when you're entertaining?" he asked, surprised that his voice was normal.

"Sometimes," she said. "Folks like some of the old romantic songs thrown in amongst the new, faster, up-beat ones."

"Such as?"

"They love George Jones," she said.

"My grandfather liked him. He loved 'Walk Through This World With Me.' What would it take in a man for you to take his hand and walk through the world with him?"

Jodie jerked her head around. "Good Lord, what made you ask that? What would it take in a woman for you to walk through the world with her?"

"I asked first," he said.

"Pretty hard question," she mumbled.

"You don't have to answer it," he said. He'd expected her to spout of a list of qualities along with acceptable alternatives.

She wanted to talk but everything she started to say

sounded contrived. For the first time in her life she was literally tongue-tied, and she hated it. "Thank you. I'll have to think about it for a while."

He covered a yawn with his hand. "I'm going to my room to send the story out on email and go to sleep. Two days of travel to get here, three days here and three more traveling days to get back to Florida. How on earth does a person do this for a whole year?"

"Kind of puts a new twist on the idea of a circuit, doesn't it?" She smiled.

His heart did one those crazy fluttering things. "It sure does. I'm glad we didn't bring my car after all. Not because of the miles but the truck is actually more comfortable for long hauls like this one coming up."

She started cleaning up the leftovers, putting chicken and potato salad in the refrigerator, rolls back in the plastic bag, paper napkins in the trash can. "How long will the story take tonight?"

"Not very. It's for the newspaper. Got the magazine article done in San Antonio and they don't need another one until we do the Houston rodeo. Newspaper is what, when, who, and how with just a bit of commentary."

"Then good night. What's on for tomorrow?" she asked.

"I figured you'd tell me. Yuma has a lot to offer. We missed the parade earlier today but there are other things. Or we can skip over the line to Los Algodones in Baja."

"Or we can laze around the pool. Lord, ain't it nice to be able to swim outside in February? I've always wondered why on Earth Valentine's Day is in February. We've all got runny noses and chapped lips and it's a lover's holiday. Don't make a bit of sense to me. Candy and flowers. Candy when our stomachs are already touchy with the flu and flowers to set off another bout of sneezing," she said.

He grinned at her tirade.

She wondered why she'd never been attracted to blond-haired men.

He waved at the door. "Good night, Jodie. We'll go over to Baja tomorrow and do some shopping, maybe eat at a Mexican cantina or something local."

"Sounds wonderful," she nodded. God, why couldn't they have a rousting good fight over anything at all? It didn't matter if it was whether the chicken was crispy enough or the hotel maid was pretty or ugly. Something so she could hate him rather than want to kiss him goodnight. She wasn't going to fall for him, not even if they were thrown together in close proximity for the next six weeks. Mixing their two lifestyles would be worse than what Roseanna and Trey had done. That their marriage was working this second time around was a pure miracle.

She took a quick shower, scrubbing her arm again. The skin looked normal after a good dousing of moisturizing lotion but the wrist still moved looked like it had a steel rod poked up through the middle. She did the exercises the doctor had suggested and went to bed. At two o'clock she finally drifted off to sleep, only to dream of being bucked off a big, mean, brown bull named El Diablo. In her dream she dusted herself off, raised both her arms showing everyone she was fine, and then crumpled into a heap right there in the middle of the arena. She awoke at daybreak in a sweat. Was the dream a prophecy telling her that she'd die if she ever rode again? She shook away the gloom and doom and opened the drapes to let in sunlight. At least the sky wasn't gray and cloudy.

It was just a nightmare, nothing more.

Jimmy was haggling with a merchant for a tapestry. Jodie ignored him and looked through a stack of *serapes*. The price was less than half what she'd seen them for in Oklahoma and Texas. They were wonderful to throw over a jacket or even a heavy coat for chores on really cold days. She picked out half a dozen and carried them to the front where Jimmy and the man finally reached an agreeable price on the tapestry.

"How much?" she asked.

"American dollars?" He narrowed his eyes and assessed the woman's worth.

She nodded.

He named a price, and she picked the stack up and started to return them to the shelf at the back of the store.

"Whoa! Wait a minute lady. We can talk about this. You are buying six. I will give you a discount for buying so many," he said in broken but understandable English.

"How much?"

He quoted a price and the haggling began. She offered him half that. They finally agreed on a price in the middle. He threw up his hands saying that his family would have to go hungry that night since the Anglo had robbed him.

A pretty woman with long, straight, black hair, ebony eyes, and skin the color of caramel pushed back a curtain with a chuckle. "Oh, Papa, you know your family has never been hungry. Madre says to come into the kitchen and have your beans and chalupas. I'll take care of the business here."

She settled quickly with Jodie and then the flirting began. She batted her lashes at Jimmy and enticed him to buy wallets. He purchased two without haggling. Talked him into a serape because it had a stripe exactly the color of his eyes. He paid the full price.

Jodie stood at the door with her sack of serapes and fumed.

"Perhaps you would like for me to show you the rest of Los Algodones? There is much that the tourists cannot see but I could guide you, then we could have supper together. Madre is making tamales tonight. She would like to meet you. Your sister can go on and shop wherever she wants and meet you back at your hotel, no?"

Jodie cleared her throat. If the woman got any closer to Jimmy she'd have to hire a surgeon to separate them.

Jimmy glanced her way but only briefly. Then he and the señorita began a conversation in rapid Spanish that Jodie couldn't follow. There was much laughing and gesturing, and at one point, she thought for sure that little hussy was going to kiss him right on the lips.

Then suddenly she picked up a piece of paper and rustled through the cash register for a pencil. He signed his name with a flourish and handed it to her. She held it to her heart and all but swooned right there in the floor of the shop.

"What in the hell was that all about?" Jodie asked when they got out of hearing distance.

"She went over to Yuma with her boyfriend and saw a movie. She thought I was the star and was determined I'd stay in town and have supper with her family. It would be an honor to have a movie star at their table. It would make them all very important."

"And you fell for that line? She was going to get rid of me, knock you in the head, and steal all your money," Jodie said.

"Come on, you're just jealous because she didn't think you were Julia Roberts. Besides, I've been mistaken a few other times for Matthew McConaughey. She wanted my autograph anyway even if I wasn't Matty old boy. She was sure she'd seen me in some movie."

"God, your ego is surpassed only by your—"

"What?" His voice held a cutting edge. "You want to tell me you didn't have an ego when you won that big gold buckle five years ago? Didn't you sign a few autographs for little kids?"

"Sure I did, but not for a good-looking man who was fawning all over me. If it had been kids flirting with you, it would have been one thing. That was not a kid, darlin'," she said sarcastically.

He took her arm and guided her into a coffee shop. Already in a temper fit, she was further aggravated by her own reaction to his touch on her bare skin. She shook him away and told the lady behind the counter that she'd have a triple latte with whipped cream. Thank goodness the woman was round as a turnip and didn't try to impress Jimmy by asking for his autograph.

"Did that woman think you were Matthew too?" she asked when he brought the coffee to the table she'd found.

"No, she didn't. She's so old she probably never goes to the movies."

"Hmphhh," she snorted.

"Are you jealous?"

"Hell, no!"

"I would have sworn I saw a little green in the store when Isabella invited me to dinner," he said.

"Of course you did. If anyone is going to get fresh

tamales, it should be me. You don't even like good food. I bet you've got a decaf with skim milk in that cup right now." She tried to cover truth with bravado.

"What can I say? You know me." He threw up both hands. The woman had been itching for a fight all day.

"You can say I'm wrong that you've got pure whipped cream and real coffee, maybe even espresso," she said.

"But it's not. It's decaf with skim milk just like you said. But if you don't stop being cantankerous, I'm going to take you back to the hotel and come back here for supper with the señorita."

"Oh?" She cocked her head to one side. "It's my truck and it's not coming up to the parking lot out there and it's sure not coming across the border."

"Ever hear of a taxi? It's only nine miles from our hotel over here. I'm sure it wouldn't cost that much. Probably be a deal since I'd get a free supper out of it."

"That might not be all you get," she retorted.

"Is this a lovers' spat?" he asked.

High color filled her cheeks. She covered it by leaning forward to sip coffee and letting her hair fall over her face. "We would have to be lovers for that, now wouldn't we? You're talking to the woman who speaks English, not the pretty little Maria who spits out fast Spanish."

"We did have that one kiss. Maybe we're destined to be more than colleagues," he said.

"That kiss was a major mistake," she said.

"We'll see." He got the last word.

But only because her head was spinning. She'd wanted a good old fight and she'd gotten it. Now she could go back to the job of judging bulls and riders and forget about him. His ego would keep her from ever falling for him. That look in his eye and the posturing for the young storekeeper would always be there to set her on the right path if she had a crazy notion that she'd like to kiss him again. Right at that moment she would have rather drenched his high-dollar white silk shirt with her latte than feel his lips on hers.

Sure you would, her conscience argued. *Right now you've never wanted to embrace him more. If you're honest you were so jealous of that woman, you would have liked to have snatched her bald.*

She stoically ignored the niggling voice and sipped her coffee. It was a lovely, sunny day. No clouds in the gorgeous blue sky. James Moses Crowe was not going to spoil one more minute of it. And she wasn't even going to think about kissing him.

That idea lasted all of two seconds, vanishing when he smiled.

Chapter Ten

J odie sat on the white sugar sand at Panama City Beach, Florida, and watched the sun set at the end of the ocean. Sea oats waved in the gentle breeze; the same wind picked up wisps of her hair, blowing it across her face. She deftly pulled it back into a ponytail at the nape of her neck. The wrist exercises had already begun to work wonders. Not that she had full range of motion yet, but in less than a week she could already see a difference.

She was more exhausted by the time they reached the Sugar Sands Motel than she'd been on the whole trip, but then she'd expected to be. This leg was one of the worst. From San Antonio to Yuma was over a thousand miles, and from Yuma to Panama City Beach was more than eighteen hundred miles. They still had four hundred to do the next day before they reached Kissimmee. Three days there and then there was a four-day break before they had to be in Dade City at the Pasco County Fair and Championship Rodeo for one night only and then on to Davie for two days. At least they'd be able to rest after the Kissimmee stopover because after Davie it was back to Houston and that was another thousand miles.

She sighed. Maybe she was getting too old for this.

"Twenty-six isn't old," she said aloud, but only the wind answered.

Finally, she admitted that the physical trip wasn't as tiring as the mental one. Making the decision not to fall for Jimmy had been easy; carrying it out was a whole heck of a lot more difficult. She still got angry when she thought of the pretty little señorita and every day she told herself that a relationship in which jealousy had any part was not a healthy one.

She felt his presence even before he sat down beside her in the sand, still warm from the day's allotment of sun. Before he spoke her heart did that little half step that said, *I like this man a lot. Can't you wake up and take notice of what I see and hear and think?*

"Pretty sunset," he said.

"Mmmm," she agreed without speaking.

"I'm caught up on everything now. Even the first half of my mystery novel has been sent to my agent. The last portion just needs a few details written in to make it all fit," he said.

"Congratulations," she said, and meant it.

"Today is Valentine's Day. I bought you something," he said.

She'd forgotten that it was a holiday. Roseanna had mentioned it earlier in the week, saying that she and Trey were joining Stella and Rance, Dee and Jack, and Greta and Kyle for dinner at a restaurant in Ardmore.

Jimmy handed her a big heart-shaped box of assorted chocolates. "It's not anything fancy but every place else that sold candy was closed when I drove into town for supplies. I found one grocery store still open and everything there was picked over."

She swallowed hard and fought back tears. "This is so sweet. You are a good friend. Thank you."

A good friend? That was a beginning, he guessed.

She tore the cellophane wrapper from the outside and opened the lid. After careful deliberation she chose a dark chocolate and closed her eyes in appreciation when she bit into it. "My favorite. Maple cream with dark chocolate. You pick one."

"They are for you," he said.

"It's Valentine's Day. Come on, share with me. Chocolate you eat on Valentine's Day is not fattening. It has no calories or fat grams and it won't make you sick," she said.

He laughed and picked out one from the center of the box. "Mmmm. Milk chocolate with lighter chocolate inside. Very good."

She ate two more before she laid back in the sand, not caring if it sifted into her hair and down her shirt. The sound of the ocean blended with the seagulls, who'd no doubt love to peck away at her box of candy. Somewhere on the west end of the beach two children giggled, one higher pitched and younger sounding than the other. An older couple appeared on the east end—a tall man with graying hair and a thin mustache and a lady in bright floral Capri pants. Both of them were barefoot and they held hands, talking in low tones as they passed Jimmy and Jodie.

Life all around her. Some beginning with a bright future. Some coming to an end with a good past. Where did she fit into the scheme of things? And why since Jimmy Crowe kissed her had she been so philosophical? For great pities sake, she was twenty-six and she had been kissed before.

"So what do you want to do for five days in between Kissimmee and Dade City? We're close to Orlando. Want to do Disney World?"

"Do you?"

"Not really. Been there. Done that. Got an old worn out T-shirt in the attic somewhere to prove it," he said.

"Do they keep everything of yours?" she asked.

"Probably. I've been pampered, I'll admit it, Jodie. But it doesn't mean that I'm weak. We are all strong-willed people. I'm just as cantankerous as they are when I think I'm right. Grandmother says I'm exactly like

Grandfather. Mother agrees except when I make a big mistake. Then I'm showing traits of my father."

"What was he like?"

"I was only five but I remember him laughing a lot and playing with me in the yard. I used to build great stories about him. He wasn't really dead. They'd just told me that to make me forget him. Someday he'd come and steal me away. When I grew up, I admitted he was gone."

"What did he look like?"

"Me. Even Grandmother agrees on that. Other than my green eyes and height, I'm his image."

"He was a short man?"

"No, just not as tall as I am. About Mother's height, I'd guess."

She reached for another piece of candy and pointed for him to help himself. She should have bought a box of assorted chocolates last month. They loosened his tongue better than a bottle of wine.

"What do you want to do during our five-day break?" she asked.

"I just had a week at home. Thought maybe you might like to fly to Sulphur for a quick visit. We could catch a red eye after the last event, rent a car, and be there by breakfast. I can rent a hotel room and work on the book, and you can have a visit."

Her eyes widened in disbelief. She was so homesick

she could cry but she wasn't about to admit it. Jodie Cahill wasn't weak either—at least on the outside.

"I'd like that," she said simply.

"Good, I'll call Cathy and have her set up the arrangements," he said.

"But you won't stay in a hotel. We've got lots of room in both the lodge and the house. I stayed in your home so you can stay in mine."

"Need to check with your family first?" he asked.

"No, we'll surprise them. Now, change back to original subject. Why did you think your father wasn't dead? Didn't you go to the funeral?"

"No, Grandmother said children didn't attend such things. She hated him. He and Mother fought over the move to the ranch, and Grandmother had begged her to leave him and come home. I remember that much very well. She'd get mad and tell him that she'd left everything for him and he could make a better effort. He'd tell her that she knew what he was when she eloped with him. I hated it when they fought. But that day they had a doozie and then she took me to a school function and when we got home he was dead. That's one reason I hate jeans. It was the first time I ever wore them and my father was dead. I blamed the jeans for years."

She couldn't imagine living with anyone twenty-four hours a day, seven days a week without fighting, and he'd just admitted that he hated confrontation.

"What are you thinking? Your brow is wrinkled like it is when you are judging," he said.

"Nothing," she said. How could she explain to him that anything worth having is worth fighting tooth, nail, hair, and eyeball for? Evidently his mother and father didn't have that kind of love. She'd grown up with two tough parents who disagreed on many occasions but it had made the marriage stronger not weaker.

Don't judge his situation by your own half bushel, Granny Etta's words haunted her and were as plain as if she were sitting right beside her on the beach. She remembered the day she'd asked Etta what she meant by that adage.

"It means that you don't have all the facts and probably never will so you can't use your own knowledge, family, or background to judge another person. You've got a half bushel of sense but it's not to be used to compare someone else's situation. Do you understand?" Etta had asked her that day.

"I think so," a much younger Jodie had replied. An older one enjoying the calm sloshing of the water as it washed in and out understood it much better.

He reached for another candy. "One more and I'm quitting. I'll have an inner tube around my middle like Grandfather did. I've been doing all the talking this evening. Tell me about you, Jodie."

"Born twenty-six years ago in Ardmore, Oklahoma.

Lived in Sulphur my whole life. Plan on dying there. Pretty simple."

The wind picked up speed and a solid bank of black clouds appeared out of nowhere. One lightning bolt and a rumble of thunder was all the warning they got before enormous rain drops poured from the sky. Jimmy grabbed Jodie's hand, and they ran back to their rooms. Jimmy had rented cabana rooms with patio doors that opened right out onto the beach. Even though the distance was only a few yards, they were soaked by the time they reached their doors.

"My candy!" she wailed as the ocean waves claimed the heart-shaped box washing it out to sea.

He shivered as he unlocked first her door and then his. "It was almost empty."

"I wanted to save the box," she said.

"I'll buy you another one," he told her. No way was he sprinting in the cold February rain and lightning to fight the ocean for a paper box of ruined candy.

"Some gentleman you are," she said.

He held the door for her. "A smart one not a foolish one."

When she turned around to smart off to him he was already gone. She could hear him mumbling through the wall separating their rooms and was glad they didn't have a connecting door. She went straight to the bathroom and turned on the water. Her mouth watered for another piece of chocolate. For that alone she battled the urge to walk across the patio they shared, march into his room and start an argument. He should have had the forethought to pick up the box when the rain started.

What exactly are you fighting against? And why are you looking for reasons to not like that man? her heart asked. Had it been blessed with a real voice, Jodie expected it would have been screaming at her.

"He's not for me. It's only because we are together all the time that I find him remotely desirable. If we'd grown up on the connecting farms, I'm sure we would have hated each other," she said.

She had one towel wrapped securely around her head and one around her body when the phone rang. She sat on the edge of the bed and answered it. "Hello."

"Get some clothes on and come on over here. While I was out I bought food and a movie. Picked up a DVD player at the hotel office," Jimmy said.

"How do you know I don't have clothes on, and what makes you think I want to watch a movie?" she asked.

"You do love to argue, don't you? My bathroom is right on the other side of the wall. I can hear the shower. I waited until it stopped before I called but I didn't give you enough time to get dressed. That's how I know. It's been four hours since you ate, and I'm sure the candy is the only thing that saved you from dying of pure starvation so you have to be hungry. That's how I know. I thought you might like a movie because you mentioned

last week that you hadn't had time to see *Wild Hogs.*
Anything else before you put on your pink jogging suit?"

"Think you're so smart, don't you?"

"I bought shrimp from a vendor outside the grocery
store. Crab boil is in the pot and I'm dropping in tiny
red potatoes and corn on the cob right now. Next the
shrimp go in. How long are you going to be?"

"Five minutes and don't you overcook that shrimp."
She'd pulled the suit, along with underpants and a bra,
from her suitcase as she talked. If she'd had anything
else to lounge around in, she would have worn it just to
prove him wrong.

The pot on the two-burner stove had been used many,
many times judging from the dents and misfitting lid
but neither Jodie or Jimmy cared. He dipped the food
from the aromatic boiling water and piled it into a bowl
that didn't match either one of the plates he'd found in
the kitchenette's cabinet.

"Want to watch the movie while we eat or after?"

She tucked a jar of cocktail sauce in the crook of her
elbow and twisted the cap off with her right hand. "While
we eat or it'll be so late we'll both fall to sleep during it."

He put the movie into the DVD player and adjusted
the volume on the television set. Then he piled his plate
as high as she had. "Leave room for cheesecake. What
do you want to drink?"

"Dr. Pepper," she said.

He pulled one regular and a diet from the refrigerator and carried them to where she sat on the floor. Her back was against the foot of the bed, her knees serving as a table for her plate, water still dripping down her back from wet hair, and no makeup. He thought she was absolutely stunning.

She popped a small potato in her mouth and peeled several shrimp while she chewed. "This is scrumptious," she said between bites. "A perfect Valentine's dinner for two."

"Even though the ocean ate your candy?"

"But we have cheesecake so all is well."

A grin split his face and his dimples deepened. The woman could get under his skin worse than anyone he'd ever met, and turn right around and make his heart and soul float like they were riding on clouds. One thing was for sure, there was never a dull moment with her. Jodie, grown up, was as sassy as Jodie, little girl. He loved both even if he never did a thing about it.

After the last shrimp was eaten, the movie finished, and the dishes stacked in the sink, he walked her from his room, across the patio and to her sliding glass doors. "I enjoyed the evening, Jodie."

"Me too. I can't think of a Valentine's Day when I had so much fun," she said.

It was one of those moments when his soul flitted about on a cloud. He took a step forward, tucked his fist beneath her chin, and leaned in for the kiss. She tasted like Dr. Pepper, cocktail sauce, and chocolate swirl cheesecake.

She wasn't ready for the kiss and hadn't prepared herself for the shock of it. Just like the first one, she had the instant feeling that her soul and body had separated. The body enjoyed the kiss. The soul was dancing on raindrops.

"I'm not so sure we should do that again," she said breathlessly when it ended.

"I'm very sure we should. Good night, Jodie," he whispered softly.

Shivers played chase up and down her backbone and it had nothing whatsoever to do with the cool night air.

Chapter Eleven

Jodie almost swooned when Roseanna drove into the driveway of the Cahill ranch house. She hadn't realized how homesick she truly was until Jimmy mentioned flying home for a few days. Rosy had met her at the airport and driven her home.

"Glad to be back?" Roseanna asked as she parked.

"You'll never know." Jodie stepped out into the howling north wind, bitter cold and with the smell of snow. She turned her face away from the gale, fighting it to get inside the warm house. She wouldn't complain if the snow was a foot deep by supper time, she was so glad to be home.

The aroma of frying sausage, eggs, hot biscuits fresh from the oven, and hot maple syrup met her when she swung open the door. She threw her coat over a rocking chair near the blazing fireplace and went straight to the kitchen.

She wrapped her mother and father into a three-way hug and inhaled deeply. God, it was good to be home. If she hadn't given her word to serve as judge, she'd be tempted to call off the rest of the tour. Hotels, restaurants, and hours of riding weren't nearly as exciting as they had been when she was younger.

"Where's Jimmy?" Bob Cahill asked.

"Change of plans at the last minute. There was some kind of business in San Antonio that he needed to be at. I didn't understand the whole thing but he caught a connecting flight out of Dallas, and we'll meet back there on the twenty-third. Lord, I've missed y'all. Is breakfast about ready?"

"It sure is. Rosy, you eating with us?" Bob asked.

Roseanna reached for a stack of plates and set the table. "You bet I am. Trey has some early morning thing at the school so he's already gone."

"So fill us in," Bob said after grace was asked.

"Not much to tell. We travel. We eat lots of fast food. We sleep and we work. I'm almost glad I'm not doing a year's worth of this, Daddy," Jodie said as she ate.

"And what about that time in San Antonio?" Roseanna asked.

"I've got a whole new respect for the time you were married to Trey the first time. The rich and shameless live a different lifestyle than we do. I got along with the staff a lot better than the relatives. Enough about that. I want to hear about home. Are Melanie and Jim getting settled in? Are the girls in school here yet? What's going on with Greta and Kyle and the rest of the gang?"

A company limo waited for Jimmy at the airport. He lounged back and shut his eyes, catching a brief nap on the way to the office building in downtown San Antonio. He really didn't want to be in Texas right now and couldn't imagine what kind of business was so pressing he had to attend the meeting. Cathy was evasive when she relayed the message from his mother and grandmother, refusing to give any details.

He combed his hair with his fingers in the mirrored walls of the elevator and rubbed the sleep from his eyes. *What was Jodie doing right now? Would she and Roseanna have reached the ranch?* He'd offered to rent a car for her but she'd refused, saying that her sister would come to the airport and deliver her back to it. She'd be back to the flight waiting area at the right time to board the plane and fly back to Florida in five days.

A familiar ding let him know he'd reached the penthouse floor. The doors opened at the end of the conference room. A long, narrow mahogany table with legs big enough to support the second floor of a mansion surrounded by twelve chairs occupied the middle of the floor. Three walls were paneled in a rich red wood. The fourth was a solid expanse of glass overlooking San Antonio. The sky was gray that morning with a hazy fog obliterating the view. Only four people waited: Amelia, Lorraine, Cathy, and the company's head attorney.

Amelia was her usual self in a fitted black suit with a white silk blouse and diamonds in her ears. She looked up and her expression looked like it did when Jimmy was in grade school and brought home a B on his report card.

Gold hoop earrings and a matching choker necklace complemented Lorraine's navy blue suit with gold buttons. Her attitude was almost amusing. A snide little grin tickled the corners of her mouth, and she actually reminded Jimmy of the old cat that found the bird cage open. Something was surely going on and apparently he was about to find out just what it was.

Cathy motioned toward a chair that had been pulled out for him. She was all business that morning. Charcoal gray suit, silver jewelry, notebook open in front of her.

Frowning, he greeted the women in his life with a customary kiss on the forehead for each one and took his seat beside his grandmother. "What is this all about?" he asked. Not once in the twenty-six years of his life had he been called home for a meeting in the conference room.

"I'll explain," Barry Wentz, the lawyer, said. "Unless one of you wants to lay down the foundation first."

"Just remember, James, we did what we did because we thought it was best for you," Amelia said.

"Because we wanted your life to be as uncluttered as possible," Lorraine added.

Cathy added her two cents' worth to the confusing mixture. "And because you didn't need that factor to confuse you."

Jimmy looked at the lawyer.

"Okay, as you know your mother and father were married against your grandparents' wishes. When your father died, your grandparents brought you and your mother back to San Antonio to live."

Jimmy nodded. So far it was just past history.

"You have more family, James, on your father's side. Your paternal grandfather has recently died in Sulphur, Oklahoma. I don't know how much you remember but that is where your father, William, was working when he died. There was a life insurance policy and you were listed as the sole beneficiary with your mother acting as trustee. In a letter he left behind he stated that he knew she would go back to her own wealth and would never need the money, but he wanted to leave you something in case he wasn't around. So first of all, the insurance policy was triple indemnity if death occurred by accident, and here it is. A copy of the policy and the check from that with the interest from the past year. You were actually entitled to it on your twenty-fifth birthday." He pushed a folder across the table.

Jimmy opened it, glanced at the $300 thousand dollar check and briefly scanned the insurance policy. Everything was in order.

"Now to the rest. Your paternal grandfather lived north of Sulphur on a ranch. It has a section or 640 acres of land. He died two weeks ago in a nursing home where he'd been for more than twenty years. The ranch is grown up from the aerial photographs we've had taken. It's got an old three-bedroom frame house on it but no doubt it's in dire need of repairs. No one has lived in it since your parents lived there briefly with you when your grandfather first went to the nursing home, and that was twenty-one years ago. He's left the ranch to his only grandson, which is you. I suggest we put it on the market this week. There's also another insurance policy which will amount to a few thousand dollars."

Jimmy felt like someone had kicked the breath from his lungs. He'd had a grandfather all these years and the knowledge had been kept from him. "Why wasn't I told about my family?" he asked tersely.

"Because I didn't want you to be around those people," Lorraine said.

"Why?"

"They were just farmers. Your grandfather fell and broke his hip so we went to that godforsaken place to help with the ranch. It was just supposed to be until your grandfather could come back to the ranch but he had a stroke and your father was killed in that accident."

"But I could have gone to see him," Jimmy said.

"Didn't you hear your mother?" Cathy said. "You didn't need to be around those people. You are too sensitive as it is."

"You knew too?" Jimmy asked.

"Of course. I take care of all your finances, remember? I knew about the trust fund and the land years ago."

"Do I have other relatives in that area?" Jimmy asked the lawyer.

"Yes. Your grandfather had a niece who lived in the house on the next farm over. From all the reports we have she was faithful enough to visit him in the nursing home on a regular basis. She and her husband leased the land for a few dollars a year and she kept an eye on the property for your grandfather. She was given power of attorney while he was living. I guess she thought he'd leave his property to her for her efforts. I hope she's not too disappointed. Her last name is Parsons. They have a son named . . ."

"Kyle," Jimmy finished for him.

"How do you know about Kyle?" Lorraine asked.

"He's a friend of Jodie's," he almost whispered. "I've had cousins and family all this time and you kept me from them. I can't believe this."

"I told you, we did what we thought was best for you. It would have been confusing for you to live in our world and visit in that one. I hated it there. You would have too," Lorraine said.

"Why are you telling me this now? You've kept the trust fund a big secret. Why tell me about the property and the fact I have family at this point? Why didn't you just keep me in the dark about that too?"

Lorraine looked him right in the eye. "Because of that woman you are traveling with. You said you were going there for a few days so she can visit her people. It might come up in conversation about your grandfather. Crowe isn't a common name even in those parts and it's a small town. Everyone knows everybody else and what their business is. We were afraid you'd find out from someone else."

"Someone would remember at some point because you look so much like William," Amelia added.

"I can't believe you've kept all this from me," he mumbled.

"Grow up," Cathy said. "If you weren't so weak, it wouldn't have been necessary. You are twenty-six. It's time you put away your toys and entered the adult world. We can use you in the corporation but you're out there playing writer. There's no future in that, James. Call the realtor. Sell the land. Forget about the past, and we'll give you an office with a lovely view."

Jimmy looked at the lawyer. "This land. It's mine. My name only and no one else's? And the money is mine?"

"That's right. I have two real estate agents ready. You can go over their contracts and see which one you want to use. Here are the deeds, tax reports, and all the financial papers. The section of land is adjacent to his niece's ranch. I wouldn't expect to make a lot of money from it since it hasn't been taken care of properly all these years."

Jimmy gathered all the papers together. "It's not for sale."

"Whatever are you going to do with land in that . . ."

Jimmy gave his mother a look that stopped her mid-sentence. "First of all I'm going to look at it, and second I'm going to call Kyle Parsons and ask him to round up everyone I might be kin to so I can meet them. After that I'll make a decision."

"You don't have to take that tone," Cathy said.

Jimmy shot her a go-to-hell look. "Thank you, Mr. Wentz, for making me aware of all this. Good day, Mother, Grandmother, and Cathy."

Amelia shot up in a blast from her chair. "Where do you think you are going?"

"I'm twenty-six. I don't think I have to answer to anyone of you anymore," he said.

Lorraine stood up so fast she knocked her chair over. It fell with very little noise on the thick carpet. She shoved her face toward Jimmy until their noses were barely two inches apart. "You are acting like your worthless father. What do you think you'll do? Go there and ranch? Great God. I can just see it. You out there pulling up stumps and plowing in custom-tailored suits and seven hundred dollar shoes. Wake up, James! You have not been groomed to be a dirt farmer."

"Did I have a choice in that?" he asked.

She slapped the table in a rare show of emotion. "At five years old, no! You did not have a choice. I did what was best for you."

He picked up the papers and started toward the elevator doors. "Thank you. I'm not five years old anymore so now I'll do what's best for me."

"If you walk out of here with that attitude, you can stay gone," Amelia said with icy composure. "We are a family and we'll discuss the best way to handle this situation for all concerned. You don't need to be strapped down with some worthless Oklahoma land. God Almighty, you aren't thinking like a Fleming. You're acting like that hotheaded father of yours."

Jimmy didn't even look back when he stepped inside the elevator.

Jodie was too excited to sleep that morning. She helped her father with the outside chores, spent an hour at the lodge with her sister and brother-in-law, and helped out by making a peach cobbler for the guests' supper that evening. By the time she got back to the house Joanna was putting on her coat to go grocery shopping, so she went along. They met and talked with several acquaintances in the store, catching up on local gossip. On the way back to the ranch, Jodie leaned back and sighed. This was exactly what she needed: some time away from Jimmy to get her bearings. She had them now. She was

Jodie Cahill, back at home in Murray County. Nothing in the next six weeks could shake that again.

They'd unloaded all the food and were busy putting it away when Granny Etta and her friend Roxie dropped by to see Jodie. Etta wore a red sweatshirt with a heart embroidered on the front with her blue jeans. Roxie was decked out in a cherry-red velour sweatsuit and high heeled red demi-boots. Her bright red hair was ratted up in one of her signature hairstyles.

Etta put on a pot of coffee. "You hear about Ratch Crowe dyin' while you were gone?" she asked Jodie.

"Who is Ratch Crowe?"

"Oh, you probably wouldn't remember him. He's been in the nursing home since you were in kindergarten. Wasn't it about that long, Roxie?"

"Yep, he came sniffing around my boarding house right before that. His wife died a year or so before. I got to say, he did wait the right amount of mourning time before he tried to court me. But Lord have mercy, I just plain wasn't interested," Roxie said.

Jodie smiled as she set out a platter of her mother's oatmeal cookies. "So you two have had to fight off the gentlemen callers a time or two in your day?"

"Every eligible woman in Murray County had to tell Ratch to go home once the proper year was over," Etta said.

"What was wrong with him?" Jodie asked.

"He was just lookin' for a woman to take care of him

like Novaline did," Joanna said. "I remember when his son left these parts. Right out of high school. Sick of the farm. Went out to West Texas to work. Anyway, Ratch was a hard man. Told that boy if he didn't stay on the farm he wasn't to come back. He didn't even let him know when his mother died. It wasn't until Ratch fell and broke his hip that he called his son home and that's when he found out his mother was dead."

Jodie poured coffee for four and sat down to listen to the story. "Some family. What happened?"

"Well, the son brought his family and came home to help out. They'd put Ratch in the nursing home for some rehabilitation, but then he had a stroke and it looked like he was going to be there a long time. The son, what was his name?" Etta put a finger to her cheek trying to remember.

"Wilbur? William?" Roxie asked.

"They called him Bud," Joanna remembered. "The newspaper said he'd been preceded in death by his son, William. And then it had Bud in parentheses. So I guess everyone who might remember him would remember the nickname."

"That's right," Etta said. "Ratch had the stroke. Bud had only been here a few weeks and he had an accident and died. His family went on back to Texas where they come from and no one ever heard from them again."

Jodie brushed cookie crumbs from her green plaid flannel shirt.

"And Emma Ponders died. You remember her, Jodie?"

"Miss Emma, who lived up behind the school?"

"That's her. She and Ratch both died the same day. Nursing home lost two of their oldest patients in less than twenty-four hours. Etta, how old would Ratch's son be now if he was still alive?" Roxie asked.

"Well, Ratch and Novaline were both past forty when they had that boy. Didn't think they were ever going to have children. Let's see, Ratch was ninety so Bud would be in his late forties if he was alive," Etta said.

"Whatever happened to the family he left behind?" Joanna asked.

"The wife and kid or was it kids, I can't remember right now. Anyway, they went home to her people. Never heard anything about them again."

Suddenly Jodie's brain began to connect the dots. "Crowe? Did you say this old man's name was Crowe and he lived around here?"

"That's what we've been telling you, child. He was Kay Parson's uncle. Kyle's great uncle. She visited him in the nursing home every week. Ratch's body was all messed up with the broke hip and the stroke, which got the other side, but they said his mind was still sharp. Kay and Billy leased the ranch from him for a few dollars a year and she kept an eye on things. Wonder what they'll do with that ranch? Ratch might have left it to Kay and that would be the smart thing. I'm sure those people in Texas wouldn't want it. They never came back here the whole time to see about the old man. It might go on the market. You got enough in your bank account for a down payment, Jodie?" Etta asked.

"What was this Bud's wife's name?" she asked.

"Here I am telling you all about a ranch that's coming up for sale, and you've been chomping at the bit for more'n a year about having your own place and you're interested in Ratch's daughter-in-law? What is the matter with you? You got too much rodeo dust in your brain?" Etta asked.

"Crowe? Is that C-R-O-W-E?"

"That's right," Roxie said.

Jodie hopped up to answer the doorbell when it rang and swung the door open to find Jimmy standing on the other side. The bewildered look in his dark green eyes caused her to step back and motion him inside.

"I'd like it better if you came out and took a ride with me," he said.

She reached for her coat.

"Momma, I'll be back in a little while!" she called out toward the kitchen.

"What has happened? You look like you lost your best friend or saw a ghost." she asked when they were inside the rental car he'd picked up at the Dallas airport.

"It's a long story," he said.

"I've got all the time in the world. One question. Was Ratch Crowe your grandfather?"

He nodded.

Chapter Twelve

Jimmy started the engine and drove to the end of the lane, then stopped. He had no idea which way to go. He assumed north because the attorney had mentioned the ranch being north of Sulphur. "Do you know Kay Parsons?" he asked.

"Of course. That's Kyle's mother," Jodie said. She'd kept her silence after asking him if Ratch was his grandfather, giving him time to talk, but it hadn't been easy.

"Do you know where they live?"

"Turn north," she pointed.

She gave directions and he followed them right up to a long, low brick house with a porch wrapped around three sides. A split log fence circled the house and cows stuck their heads through the rails to nibble at the grass in the yard.

He stopped the car and stared ahead as if in a stupor.

"Want to tell me why we're here?" she asked.

"These people are my relatives and I don't know them. I never knew my grandfather, Ratch Crowe. That's a strange name, isn't it? I just found out this morning. They kept it from me for my own good, they said."

His sentences were delivered in monotone.

"Why did they tell you now?"

"Because I was coming here to stay at the lodge or your house and they thought I might hear his name in conversation. Will you go with me to talk to Kay?"

"Of course. I've known the family my whole life. Kyle and my sister Roseanna dated a while back before she married Trey the first time," Jodie said.

He opened the door slowly as if dreading the meeting.

Jodie slung the gate to one side then closed it after they were inside the yard. She was the one who knocked heavily on the door frame. She was tempted to take Jimmy's hand in hers for support but was afraid of the emotions the touch would create.

"Yes?" Kay answered the door. She wore jeans and an orange sweatshirt. Her salt and pepper-colored hair was held away from her face with a wide headband. Flour dotted her forehead but her fingernails were freshly polished in bright red. "Don't just stand out there in the cold, Jodie. Come on in here. I'm making blackberry cobbler for supper. Kyle and Greta are coming over, and she's partial to cobbler with ice cream. Who's this with you?"

When they stepped inside the house, Kay's hand went to her mouth. "Good Lord, it can't be. You have to be Jimmy. You are the spitting image of my cousin, Bud."

Jimmy nodded unable to say a word.

Kay wrapped him into a hug that almost took his breath away. "I told them all you'd find your way home someday and here you are. Did you know that Uncle Ratch died and left you the ranch?"

"I just found out this morning. I had no idea I had family," he said.

"I figured as much. You'll have to meet us all. Can you come for supper tonight? My daughters won't be here but Kyle will and you can meet him. He's your second cousin and married to Greta. We'll have to plan a family reunion so you can get to know the rest of your family. Come sit in the kitchen and have a cup of coffee while I finish making the cobbler."

"I think Jimmy would like to go over to the ranch if ya'll don't mind," Jodie said.

"Mind? Lord, no, I don't mind. Let me get you the key. The place will be dusty. I only go over there twice a year to do any cleaning. Ratch said in the beginning I wasn't to move a single thing. He said someday it would be important that it be the same as the day Jimmy left it. Guess he had his reasons. Anyway, here's the key. If you decide to sell it don't be listing it with a realtor, Jimmy. There's lots of family who'd buy the place and give you a fair price."

"Yes ma'am, and thank you. Were you serious about supper?" Jimmy asked.

"I sure was and bring Jodie with you. I'll keep her and Greta apart at the table so you and Kyle don't have to referee," Kay teased.

He raised an eyebrow toward Jodie.

"I'll explain later. What time?" she asked.

"We don't stand on formality, Jodie. Supper will be on the table at six. Come on around anytime before that and visit with us," Kay said.

Jimmy was still in a daze when he followed Jodie back to the dirt road and drove back to the south. A mile down the road she told him to turn left and hopped out of the car to unlock a padlock on the gate. She swung it wide so he could drive through and then closed it. A quarter of a mile up the rutted lane he found the house and memories surrounded him like a warm blanket.

"We drove up here in a pickup truck," he said. "Mother said it had better be for only a few weeks because she wasn't living like this. I couldn't understand why. There were kittens on the porch and puppies under it. A man was sitting in an old chair right there," he pointed. "He rode the other horse that was out there in the barn. I wanted to ride it but Mother said I wasn't old enough."

"You didn't remember any of this before now?" Jodie asked.

"No, I only had one memory of living here. Will you go inside with me?" he asked.

"You might want to do it alone," she suggested.

"I don't think so," he said.

She followed him to the porch where he looked at the straight-back chair, once painted white and now chipped and flaking. She suspected that he was envisioning the man who sat in the chair and helped with the farm chores. She'd have to ask Kay later who it was—someone still around or a drifter.

He opened the screen door and unlocked the wooden one. The house was cold and smelled musty but that was no surprise. It hadn't been lived in for more than twenty years. Crocheted doilies were pinned to the arms and back of a gold floral sofa on the right. Once white, they were yellowed with age. To the left was a large fireplace with wood stacked beside it. A granddaddy long-legged spider crawled lazily over the top of the logs. Two recliners faced an old floor model television set. Knick-knacks dated the room even more than the furniture. Little ducks every-where. Yellow ones. White ones. Babies. Grown ones with wings flapping. Made of wood, of porcelain, ceramic, and one of clear glass. All covered with a thin layer of dust.

Jimmy touched one and then the other. "Daddy said I could look at them but not to touch. When Grandpa came home he'd be really mad if I broke one because they'd been Grandma's collection. Strange that I would remember that now and never before."

The one memory I kept of Jodie is the one that tied me to this place, the only one that brought me back here. But why did I repress all the others?

He roamed on straight ahead through an archway into the kitchen. A wood table with four chairs surrounding it took center stage. Cabinets made a U shape around three walls. A window above the sink still had the same curtains hanging—white with a border of waddling ducks.

"There was an ivy plant in the window. Mother watered it every day. Once she told me it would die when we left. I asked her where we were going, and she said back to Texas one way or the other, that she wasn't living in this kind of place much longer."

Jodie followed him back into the living room and down the hallway. An open door to the right led into a big country bathroom. A claw-footed tub on the far end, a wall-hung sink to the left and the toilet around a partition to the right. Two wicker hampers and a chair that matched the one on the porch were scattered along the available wall space. Towels had been converted into curtains over the window above the tub. They'd been bright yellow at one time. Now where the folds had been exposed to the sun they were almost colorless.

"I loved taking a bath in the tub. I had a boat and some army men and they were constantly waging battles in there," he whispered.

Lord, what would it be like to have your past repressed and suddenly flood back with such power? She couldn't begin to imagine the feelings unfolding around him right now.

He opened a door to his left and peeped inside. "This was Grandpa's room and Daddy said I wasn't ever to go in there. Someday he'd come home and he wouldn't like it if his things were messed with. It was like Daddy didn't really like Grandpa. I wanted to touch that big old belt thing right there." He pointed to a leather strop hanging behind the door on a rusty nail.

"Did you?" Jodie asked.

"No, Daddy shut the door. His face looked sad. I remember that now. He said no child of his would ever touch that thing."

He opened another door. "Mother and Daddy's room," he said.

He gasped and sunk to the floor beside the bed.

Jodie sat beside him. "Are you all right? Is this enough for one day? Let's go, Jimmy. You are so pale, it's scaring me."

"Daddy was on this bed. They came and got me and brought me in here. He was stretched out on this bed and his breath was all raspy. He held my hand and told me to be good and then blood bubbles came out of his mouth and that man, the one who rode the other horse, took me out of the room. I was crying and the man held me in his arms until Mother came and took me in my own room," he whispered hoarsely.

Jodie noticed dark stains on the pillowcase. Evidently Kay had abided by Ratch's wishes. Nothing had been changed.

Jimmy stood up and went across the hall to the last bedroom. He pushed open the door. On the dresser lay the new pair of jeans and the Western shirt with pearl snaps. He didn't need repressed memory to know what the dark stains were on the shirt. What did come back was the memory of his mother when she removed the jeans and shirt.

"We are going home, James. I want you to forget this place. Don't ever think of it again. Your father is dead, and I want you to forget all about him. Promise me, James," she had said.

Jimmy was suddenly five years old again. He looked in the mirror at the little boy who'd just started kindergarten in Sulphur, Oklahoma. He wore nothing but his underwear, black framed glasses with thick lenses, and a raw place on his nose where that big kid had hit him at the rodeo day. When he was five, it was easy to forget the whole day as well as the whole six weeks they'd been in Oklahoma.

He blinked and Jimmy, the grown man, looked back at him with haunted eyes. "That afternoon two big black cars came up in the yard. The funeral director took Daddy away. Mother and I got into the other one, a limo Grandmother sent for us, and we went to San Antonio."

"Didn't you come back for the funeral?"

"No, there was no funeral. I do remember that. I was so young I didn't know to ask questions. We went from moving every few months to a big house and a nice school and Mother was careful to never mention anything about the past," he said.

"Mercy!" Jodie said.

"Yeah," he agreed. "Let's go unload my things. I'm staying here until we have to leave for the next rodeo."

"Hey, do you think that's a good idea? You can stay at the ranch. The lodge is full for the next few days but there're extra bedrooms at the ranch," she said.

"No, I'm staying right here. Looks like the electricity is on." He flipped a light switch on the living room wall.

"Okay, if you think that's the best. Here's the thermostat. What temperature do you want? I hope the heating unit still works. It's probably not been turned on in years," she said.

"Try sixty-eight degrees," he said.

She pushed the right buttons and a steady hum started. The curtains began to blow from the warm air flowing from floor vents and the room filled with the smell of hot dust particles.

"It always smells funny for an hour or so after you turn on the heat in the winter. Dust settles in the vents and the hot air burns them. It'll be all right in a little while," Jodie assured him.

They piled several suitcases, his laptop, and three stuffed garment bags on the sofa in the living room. Jodie wondered why on earth he'd brought so much for a five-day visit but didn't ask. She was still wandering around in a daze from the day's events. She couldn't begin to fathom what he was thinking.

That he could possibly be living in Murray County permanently was enough to rattle her into a mass of raw nerves. She'd grown to like the man far too much to have him that close. Getting past her feelings would be difficult enough with him seven or eight hours away and never seeing him again.

"What time is it?" he asked.

She pointed to an electric clock on the kitchen wall— a funny-looking ceramic duck with eyes that moved back and forth with every tick of the second hand. The cord dropped from the bottom of the clock to a plug near the baseboards.

"Five already. I won't have time for a bath before we go to Kay's for supper. Do you need to go back to the ranch to dress?"

"In these parts we don't dress for supper, Jimmy. Kay will probably still be wearing what she had on today only without the flour on her face. Greta might do a little more because she comes from the same kind of people you do," Jodie said.

"And what does that mean?" he asked.

She shook her finger right under his nose. "Hey, don't you talk to me in that tone. You might want and need a good rousting fight right now and I'm the only one here to give you one, but I'm not going to be your whipping tree, James Moses."

"Don't call me that. I'm just plain old Jimmy."

"Okay, plain old Jimmy, why don't you want to be called James Moses today?"

"Because that's not my given name. My name is James William after my father. Mother changed it to Moses after we went back to Texas. That was Grandmother's maiden name and they evidently didn't want me to have my father's name. I may legally change it back after I think about it a while."

"Don't let anger make bad choices," she said.

"I said I'd think about it," he snapped.

"Then do it with a clear mind, not while you are mad at the world and wallowing in forgotten memories. What on Earth happened in San Antonio anyway?"

"They told me. Very business-like and blunt. Then Mother got angry. I think that's what triggered my memory. I hadn't seen her that upset since the day we drove up in the front yard out there. She resented the way of life she'd gotten when she left San Antonio. I know that now. As a little kid though, I only knew she yelled a lot."

"It'll all come back. Think about it though before you

go off half cocked and make decisions you'll regret," she said.

He nervously brushed his hair back with his finger-tips. What she said made sense. "Let's go meet my cousin, Kyle, and have supper with the other side of my family. Just when I thought my world was so fixed and boring—"

"God threw a monkey wrench in it," she finished the sentence for him.

"A big one," he said.

Supper was rump roast cooked with potatoes and carrots, apple salad, green beans with bacon seasoning, and corn on the cob. The table was set with plain white stoneware dishes and serviceable stainless flatware. Iced tea glasses were pint Mason jars with handles on the sides. Kay sat at one end of the table and her husband, Billy, on the other. Greta and Kyle were on one side. Jodie and Jimmy across from them. Kyle said grace and Kay started passing dishes.

"I can't believe that you are Kyle's cousin. The world is a small place after all, isn't it? Who would've thought it when you drove up in that Mustang to get Jodie?"

"Not me," Jimmy said.

"All children come home eventually, for one reason or the other," Kay said. "Here, Jimmy, have some corn. We used to have some of those little things that stick in the ends so you can handle it better, but they all got lost.

You'll just have to get your fingers all greasy and use your napkin."

"Could you tell me about my father?" Jimmy asked.

"Sure, what do you want to know?" Billy said.

Jimmy bit into a hot roll that would rival Mohin's any day of the week. "Anything."

"He was a good man. He just wanted to find his own path. Ratch wanted him to stay on the ranch and follow in his footsteps just the way he'd followed in his father's. Bud wasn't satisfied to do that. He wanted to go to college and Ratch wouldn't have any part of it, not even after Bud got a scholarship to East Central. He said the boy didn't need any more learning than he could get on the ranch," Billy said.

"Ratch was a hard man but an honest one," Kay said in his defense. "He'd been a young man during the Depression and that always has a bearing on a person. My father wasn't as tough on us but he had a lot of the same ideas."

"So that's why Daddy ran away?" Jimmy asked.

Kay nodded. "Finished high school and took off. It was hard on Aunt Novaline. She loved that boy so much, but she held up pretty good. Always expected him to come home and kept things ready if he did. Then Ratch broke his hip and told me to call Bud. We didn't even know where he was but Ratch did. Said he'd kept track of him the whole time. Good thing by then Aunt Novaline was dead. She'd have shot him right between the eyes for withholding that from her. I made the call and the next day Bud was back at the house. A couple of weeks after that Ratch had the stroke. It affected the other side of his body, the one opposite of the broken hip. He never walked on his own again. Used a wheelchair pretty good up until he died. He talked with a slur but I could understand him.

"He told me what he wanted done and I did it. He let us lease his land but he refused to sell it to us. Told me once that it was his grandson's land. He had a picture of you all decked out in jeans and a Western shirt that he kept in his room. I've got it amongst his belongings. There's not many. A shoebox full at the most, but I'll bring them over to the house tomorrow if you want them."

"I would like that," Jimmy said. He remembered his father taking a picture of him that morning just before he took him over to the Cahill ranch for rodeo day. Someone must have found the film and had it developed.

"You really going to stay in that old house?" Greta asked.

"I really am," Jimmy said.

"Isn't it spooky? I mean, your dad died there and there's all those sad old memories. Why don't you stay at the lodge?"

"I need the memories," he said. "This is a really good supper. Mohin, my grandmother's chef, would love to compare recipes with you."

"You should meet Mohin," Jodie laughed, lightening

the heavy mood. "I thought he was going to be this wizened little old East India man, and he's a six foot six giant with a rim of red hair around his bald head. He wears jeans and boots and his name is George Mohindovitch.

Greta giggled. "But Mohin sounds so much more like a fancy chef."

"How'd you know?" Jimmy asked.

"Been there. Done that. Left it all behind. Am not sorry," she smiled brightly at Kyle.

He leaned over and kissed her on the cheek. "Took a while to convince her but she found her broken road."

After supper, coffee in the living room and another hour of visiting, Jimmy took Jodie back to the ranch. He walked her to the door and thanked her for being there with him through the day.

"Hey, you would have done the same for me," she said.

"I'm in a confusing state of pure bewilderment," he admitted. "I'm a writer. I love what I do. I make a decent living but not a filthy rich one. I could have the rich side if I wanted to work in the corporation but I don't want to work there. I don't have one single iota of knowledge about a ranch. I don't need a square mile of land but right now I don't want to give up one square inch. I'm not sure I can live in that house over there but I have to try for a few days. Everything is a muddle and I can't explain it to myself, so why am I trying to make you understand?"

She wrapped her arm around his neck. The soft curls grazing his shirt collar tickled her fingertips. She leaned in and kissed him gently at first, then deepened the kiss. Jolts of tingles raised the hair on her arms and made her heart beat so fast she thought she'd lose her breath.

"Good night, Jimmy," she said as she stepped back. "It'll all work itself out eventually. This mess wasn't made in twenty-four hours. It won't get solved in a day either."

He turned and waved over his shoulder. If he'd had to say a word after that kiss or be shot, he would have had to drop down on his knees and put his hands behind his head. Great God in heaven, what was he going to do?

Chapter Thirteen

A cold north wind played music through the bare tree limbs. Jodie pulled her coat closer to her chest and ran from the car to the house. Roxie met her at the door and the smell of food guided her to the kitchen where the rest of the group milled around as Dee put the finishing touches on supper. Grilled steaks, stuffed twice-cooked potatoes in the shell, homemade bread sliced extra thick, tossed salad, and two pecan pies keeping warm on the back of the stove.

Roxie's bright red two-story house located on Buckhorn Corner farther south of Cahill Lodge was as much home to Jodie as her own place. She'd grown up with Dee, Stella, and Roseanna, the whole lot of them playing together in one place or the other while their grand-mothers visited about their personal lives and business.

"Where is he?" Jack asked.

Jodie looked behind her. Nothing there. "Who?"

"Don't give us that innocent look. Where is Jimmy? We've all heard about him . . ."

". . . and his car," Kyle said.

". . . and how good-looking he is," Rance joined in.

". . . and how he looks at you," Trey said.

"I don't know where Jimmy is. He took me home three nights ago and went to his new ranch. I haven't seen or heard from him since," Jodie said. What she didn't say was that she hadn't slept in three nights, that every time the phone rang she crossed her fingers hoping it was him, or that she was scared to death she'd lost him with that last kiss.

Before the conversation went any further, Roxie came into the kitchen with her arm looped through Jimmy's. "Look who I found about to ring the doorbell. I believe you girls have met Jimmy and you know your cousin, Kyle. These other men are Jack Brewer, who's married to my granddaughter, Dee."

Jack held up the hand that wasn't holding a wiggling toddler. "Hello."

"And that tall fellow over there beside Stella would be Rance Harper," she said.

Rance stepped forward and shook Jimmy's hand.

"And the last one is Trey Fields, who's married to Jodie's sister Roseanna."

Trey waved from behind Rosy. "Nice to meet you at last."

"My pleasure," Jimmy said stiffly.

Dee pulled a pan of fresh hot yeast rolls from the oven and set them on the bar. "Supper is officially ready. Jack, say grace so these folks can eat."

Silence filled the room. Jimmy, along with everyone else, bowed his head but he didn't hear a word Jack said. Instead he stole sideways glances at Jodie. She wore the white cable knit sweater and long denim skirt she'd worn to dinner at Paul's. Her hair fell forward when she tucked her chin down in reverence so he couldn't see her pale green eyes. He wished he'd been able to stand closer to her so in that moment when everyone had their eyes shut he could lean over and smell her hair.

Jack said, "Amen."

Jimmy was reminded of the football stadium. Nothing but a few whispers and crying babies when the National Anthem was played, but the minute the last note blasted through the speakers, the crowd went wild. Everyone began to grab plates and talk at once.

Roxie pushed Jimmy forward. "You better elbow your way in here or this bunch will eat it all up from you."

They loaded plates and carried them to an enormous dining room table with enough room for a dinner party twice as big. Roxie presided at the end, leaving no doubt as to who was really queen of the evening. Etta took the other end. No competition. Just two queens in residence. Dee and Jack pulled a high chair from the corner and put it between them. Stella and Rance found places on the same side of the table with Roseanna and Trey moving into place right beside them. That left four places on Roxie's right. Greta and Kyle filled two, leaving Jimmy and Jodie the others.

"We're sorry to hear about your grandfather," Dee said. "I remember him coming to church when I was a little girl. Couldn't have been more than five because Roxie says that's when he went to the nursing home. They sat in the pew in front of us every Sunday. Your grandmother, Miz Novaline, snuck us candy. She called it quiet food and would drop her hand over the pew like she was stretching. When she opened it, there would be a prize. I loved it when she brought sixlets, those little round chocolate things. They were my favorite."

"Novaline was a good woman. She loved kids," Etta said.

"Thank you." Jimmy said. He would have loved to ask questions and learn more about his grandparents, but just that much created a lump in his throat that was hard to swallow past. "So tell me Kyle, how did you and Greta meet?" He changed the subject.

Laughter filled the room. Even Roxie and Etta giggled like school girls.

"That's a good dinner story," Dee said. "Go on Kyle, tell it."

"We met first when she dumped a cup of red punch on my best white Western shirt. It was at Rosy and Trey's wedding last summer. She came down here from Tulsa with her high and mighty ways looking down her nose on me like I was nothing but something that she tracked in from the barnyard soiling her high dollar shoes."

Jimmy looked across the table at Greta expecting to see her blushing and angry enough to pour her iced tea on Kyle's head. She smiled and held up a hand, swallowed and took a turn with the story.

"You've got to realize, Kyle looked down on me just as bad. You should have seen him when I had the wreck and he lost that bull. You would have thought I was the devil reincarnated."

Kyle leaned over and kissed her cheek. "You are. See the short story is that we met at the wedding and the next day she was on her way home, driving too fast like she always does and talking on her fancy little cell phone. She dropped the phone, lost control when she tried to pick it up and caused a major wreck. My pickup and cattle trailer were damaged. I lost a bull I'd saved up a year to buy and she was more concerned with breaking the heel of her shoe than showing any remorse for what she'd done."

"Oh, honey, I had plenty of remorse afterward," Greta said. "The judge gave me a choice of six months' jail time or four months' community service since it was my sixth offense. And guess who was in charge of taking me to work at the police station and bringing me home afterward, and who had control of my weekends and free time too? None other than Mr. Kyle Parsons. God has a sense of humor, Jimmy. He let us fall in love knowing that we were as mismatched as Gabriel and Lucifer."

"She's Lucifer," Kyle pointed.

She playfully slapped at him.

"They're not a bit more mismatched than Rosy and Trey and that story starts out with your cousin Kyle," Jodie said.

"Oh?" Jimmy was enjoying the easy banter.

"Yes, it does," Rosy said. "Kyle here told me that I could not, and I repeat *could not*, all in capital letters, sing at the Arbuckle Ballroom for my sister, here, when she was in Las Vegas riding for the gold buckle. We'd been seeing each other a few weeks and he thought he was going to order me around. That was the end of our dating, let me tell you."

"What happened?" Jimmy asked.

"I sang anyway, and Jodie won the buckle. Never thought of it before this minute. But if you ever ride again in the finals, I'm going to sing at the ballroom. That might have been your good luck charm."

"I'll take all the help I can get," Jodie said.

"There's more," Trey said. "I was on I-35 when my limo started acting up so my driver pulled off at the next exit which just happened to be where the ballroom is located. There was a service station but it was closed so he drove on over to the ballroom. We went inside to ask if anyone could help us. The bartender had a beef with Rosy and used me to help settle it. Seems she'd been teasing him and winning most of the time so he led me to believe she was a hooker. When I propositioned her I found out about her right hook." He rubbed his chin. "Being the gentleman that I am, I offered to take her to dinner to make amends. Four weeks later we were married and four years later we divorced."

"Then he got himself kidnapped and they sent me down here to this godforsaken place to beg Rosy to go get him. She's a crackerjack tracker," Greta said.

"She rescued me all right and I found out I still loved her. It took me all summer to convince her to believe in me again," Trey said.

"And I had to go on a cruise so they'd have to work together at the lodge," Etta laughed.

"I'm about ready for another cruise," Roxie said. "Any of you got a problem we can fix by leaving for a few months or weeks?"

"Don't look at me," Jodie said. "I'm just fine."

A prickly little tingle on his neck let Jimmy know high color was on its way to fill his cheeks and make him look like a sophomore stumbling around on his first date. "So does Kyle figure in your story, Dee?"

"No. My story is pretty simple. I wanted out of this

place so bad I thought I'd die so when the first opportunity came along in the form of Ray Suddeth, I grabbed it and eloped. Went to Pennsylvania for a few years and then one day my husband walked in and told me my marriage had been annulled, that I'd never been married all those years. I came home to Roxie. She and Tally, Bodine and Mimosa helped cure me but mostly Jack gets the credit. He and I'd been best friends our whole life and before long we realized we'd fallen in love."

"Who're Tally, Bodine, and Mimosa?" Jimmy asked.

"Mimosa is my mother. Tally is my sister, and Bodine is her daughter. And those are stories for another dinner party, or maybe a whole weekend." Dee laughed.

"You call your mother Mimosa?"

Laughter again.

Dee made a circular motion with her hand. "That's because, help me out here everyone."

Everyone chimed in. "God and General Lee have titles. Everyone else has a name."

"How did you meet Stella?" Jimmy looked across the table at Rance, a tall, dark-haired man who looked like he belonged on one of those old cigarette commercials.

"I ran into her. Or rather she ran into me. She was doing a fancy two-step with a mop and backed right into me."

"That's because he came into Brannon Inn, the place my grandmother left me when she died. She was one of the three queens as we call them. Roxie has Roxie's b and b," Stella said.

"That stands for Bed and Breakfast or Bellyachin' and Blessin's. Tonight, I'm glad to report, is a night of Blessin's," Roxie chimed in.

"Etta has the Cahill Lodge which she's recently turned over to Melanie," Stella went on. "And my grandmother, Granny Molly Brannon, died of cancer a few months ago so I inherited the Brannon Inn. This arrogant, egotistical man barged right in with his gang of merry hunters and demanded that he had rooms reserved. I thought he was the head of a terrorist gang there to kill me for the food in my freezer."

"And I thought she was the most beautiful thing in the world but she had this crazy idea that she wanted a life-time thing and I couldn't get my mind wrapped around such a commitment with anyone. Actually I wanted a mistress, not a lifetime thing or a commitment," Rance admitted. "We finally figured out we couldn't live without each other."

"So now you know everyone's love story," Jodie said.

"All but yours," he said without looking at her.

"It's not finished yet but we're all helping her get it written," Rosy said.

"Let me know when it's finished. I'd like to hear it," Jimmy tried to keep things light. He really wanted to ask if he was somewhere in the story but even with the strange twist of fate, he still adhered to the notion that he'd come to Murray County to get over Jodie, not fall for her. He'd talked to Paul the night before, and Paul had assured him over and over that he should sell the ranch and come back to San Antonio where he belonged. Sitting around the table with Jodie, her family and friends, he wondered where he did belong.

"Okay, let's grab coffee and dessert and take it to the living room," Roxie said.

Stella sat down on the arm of the sofa beside Jimmy. "So you found your broken road home, did you?"

"What?" That was the second time he'd heard those words and he wondered if it was something local.

"Don't you ever listen to country music?"

"All the time," he said.

"Rascal Flatts?"

He nodded.

"They had a song out a few years ago called 'Bless the Broken Road.' Remember it?" she asked.

"Something about . . . oh, now I get it." He grinned and the dimples deepened. "The singer talks about finding a true love along the broken road and then he says something about God blessing the broken road that led him home to her. So you think I've been on a broken road and I've come home, do you?"

"Have you?" she asked.

"I don't know, Stella. I really, really do not know but I'm figuring things out. Maybe it has been a broken road and it's come full circle back to my roots. Who knows? Time will tell."

Rance pulled up a rocking chair beside the sofa. "It

sure will. I'll tell you one thing. When I came up here from Texas and bought the ranch next to the Brannon Inn, I sure didn't think I was coming home. But I was wrong. I've blessed that broken road that led me to Stella every day since she said she'd marry me. It's late, darlin'. You about ready to go home?"

"Yes, I am. Hope to see you around Jimmy. Don't be a stranger. Drop by our place anytime. You don't need an invitation."

"Thank you," he said.

One couple at a time left until there was no one but Roxie, Dee, Jack, Jodie, and Jimmy.

"You kids can stay up until daybreak if you want to but this sweet little old lady needs her beauty rest," Roxie said with a fluff of her red hair.

"The day you are a sweet old lady has never dawned. They'll preach your funeral by lying about your age," Jodie said.

Jimmy gasped.

Roxie laughed aloud. "You'll get used to her. She speaks her mind. Thank you, darlin'. If they don't lie about my age, you march up the aisle and call the preacher a damn liar to his face. Lord, I'd rather miss getting my mansion in heaven than have everybody in this county know my true age. And if they don't paint my fingernails red and touch up my hair, you tell them I'll claw my way up out of the grave and haunt them. I'm not going to let Henry see me with gray hair.

When he left me I was a redhead and by damn I'll be one when I see him again."

Jimmy chuckled. Roxie's voice was smooth southern comfort but she looked like a barroom floozy. Yet, everyone treated her like she was the queen.

"Good night, everyone. Dee, you lock the door behind you and wrap Jaxson up when you run across to your place. Don't you be lettin' him breathe that cold night air. He'll have the pneumonia for sure."

"Yes, ma'am," Dee said.

"So you live close by?" Jimmy asked.

"Right next door in a trailer house. My husband here, the computer whiz, keeps a little pop and beer store for the fishermen."

"And bread and aspirin," Jack said good-naturedly.

"We've been thinkin' about building a house," Dee said.

"You and Jack not living in the trailer. I can't imagine it," Jodie said.

"Well, you'd better start imagining. This one little critter has taken over every square inch of space. We're either going to have to move our bed to the front yard or build something bigger, but Dee, here, doesn't want to give up the trailer because it was my grandparents' home."

"Sentimental, huh?" Jimmy asked.

"Yes, but don't you tell, Jodie, we haven't told Roxie yet, there's another one on the way and we've got to have the room," Jack whispered.

"Congratulations!" Jodie jumped up and hugged Dee.

"How old is your son?" Jimmy asked.

"He was a year old in December. I want six or eight so we're planning anywhere from eighteen months to two years between them. I suppose it is time to let the sentimentality go and build something bigger or else make Roxie an offer on this monstrosity," Dee said.

"Don't build. Move in here. It doesn't have to be a b and b. It can be a house with lots of kids and laughter. Another generation of all of us growing up here, like Lauren is in Brannon Inn and my nieces are at Cahill Lodge," Jodie said.

"See, I told you." Jack wrapped a blanket around a wiggling toddler and headed for the door.

"Makes sense," Dee said.

Jimmy looked at Jodie. "We've got an early flight tomorrow morning. You'll be ready at eight?"

"Hey, I've got one question," Dee said.

"When did you go to school in Sulphur?"

"Two days in kindergarten. School had just started and my dad died. We moved away but we actually lived here about six weeks."

"I see. And you are Jodie's age?"

He wasn't about to go to confession right here about the reason he'd wanted Jodie to go with him on this trip. "That's right."

"Were you in my room in kindergarten?" Jodie asked.

"My teacher was Mrs. Smith. She had gray hair

that she wore all wavy and wrinkles around her eyes.
She—"

"That was my teacher. I wonder why I don't remember you," Jodie said.

"It was a long time ago," he said. "Need a ride home?"

"No, I brought Daddy's truck."

"Then goodnight and thanks for a really nice evening," Jimmy said. He let himself out the door.

Thinking about the way he felt so comfortable around the table that evening, he didn't even see the lights in his rearview mirror. Not until he parked the rental car and was stepping up on the porch did he realize someone had been following him. He had the key in the lock when he heard the car door slam and turned around.

"Come on in, Jodie," he said.

She stepped inside the living room, and he shut the door behind them. "I wanted to talk to you alone before we leave."

"You going to leave me hanging high and dry and not keep on with the tour?" he asked.

"I thought about it but I gave my word I'd judge those events and I don't want to leave those folks in a bind," she said. The place didn't smell unused anymore. The aroma of his shaving lotion, fresh apples and bananas on the kitchen cabinet, and a vanilla candle burning on the fireplace mantel gave it life.

Aggravation flared in Jimmy instantly. "You'd leave me but not them?"

"I didn't come here to fight with you."

"Why did you come, then?"

"I want you to know that kiss we shared the other night. It was just a spur of the moment thing, a . . ." she stammered.

"A mercy kiss because it had been a long day? I don't need your pity, Jodie."

"Oh, forget it. I didn't want things to be all awkward and weird between us the next six weeks because we'd shared a couple of kisses," she said.

"I've kissed women before and it wasn't awkward or strange afterward. Why should this time be any different?"

"Because . . ."

Her eyes narrowed. So he hadn't felt the same way she did. Maybe it truly was a mercy kiss and the others were just products of the moment. She took two steps forward, hooked her hand behind his neck, and planted a passionate kiss on his lips. The tingles were there; the earth stood still; every nerve in her body stood on edge.

"Because it is different, and I refuse to live in tension for six weeks," she said and marched out of the house.

He touched his lips to see if they were as hot as they felt.

"Well, congratulations, because I'll be in tension the whole time," he whispered.

Chapter Fourteen

Rain fell in a soft mist the next morning when Jimmy awoke. He wanted to pull the covers up and stay in bed another hour or two, but he doubted if a phone call to the Dallas airport would hold a flight on that excuse. Sitting on the side of the bed he propped his elbows on his knees and his face in his hands. The book was finished. In five days he'd put in all the finishing touches, polished the prose one more time, checked all the grammar, and printed it. Yesterday afternoon, on the way to dinner at Roxie's place, he'd put it in the mail.

The ranch had given him solitude and quietness to finish the job. Or was it his grandfather's spirit still lurking around, trying to lure him back to Murray County where one side of his family lived? Now it was off to six more weeks of newspaper and magazine articles about rodeos and bull riding.

And Jodie Cahill.

With a moan, he trudged into the bathroom and shaved. Afterward he finished packing and toted his luggage out to the rental. His things took up the entire trunk. Jodie would have to put hers in the back seat, but then she traveled lightly. He was the one with the baggage.

"Both mental and physical," he mumbled.

He sat for a long time looking at the small white frame house. What would his life have been like if his father hadn't died here? Would his mother in her discontentment finally given up hope and left him? Questions that had no answers plagued him as he backed up and headed off the property.

The cell phone in his shirt pocket started to ring before he'd gone a mile. He figured it was Jodie since it was already eight o'clock and he was doomed to be ten minutes late.

"Hello, I'm on the way," he answered.

"Well, that's good news." It was Cathy's voice on the other end.

"I thought you were Jodie," he explained.

"I expected as much. I called to tell you that we've given you your five days to pout and whine and check out the life of a farmer. That's all you get."

"What are you talking about?"

"Just what I said. It's over, James. Grandmother won't

do the calling, neither will Lorraine, but I will. I know what's best for you. Always have. Always will. I've booked you a flight from Dallas to San Antonio. Your little bull rider can go on to Orlando because she has to claim her vehicle. It's her decision whether she does the rest of this tour. You aren't going to join her no matter what. You are coming home and giving up this crazy writing notion. The firm needs you and you will step up to the plate and do what is required."

"And who died and made you lord and master?" Jimmy asked brusquely.

"Don't get snide. You've had your time to brood and you know I'm right. I've called the decorators for your office. It's next to mine by the way, and I've hired two secretaries for you. One is window dressing. The other is a veteran who'll take care of things."

"No."

"What does that mean? You want to hire your own secretaries? Well, then get your rear end back home and you can fire the window dressing and hire whomever you please."

"No, I'm not coming back and doing your bidding," he said.

"Do you know what the consequences are?"

"I'm sure you are about to tell me," he said.

"Yes, I am. Your expense account is shut down. I will not be available to book flights, make reservations or take care of you, darlin'. You will have to live totally on what you can make with your little hobby and what's in your checking and savings accounts."

Thank God you don't have access to that, he thought as he pulled up into the yard and Jodie came out, toting two suitcases.

"I've always paid back my bills on my expense account whenever I got paid for my writing," he said.

"Well, as of this minute, you'll pay as you go if you want to run around playing instead of doing some real work," she said. "Don't be a fool, James. You've been spoiled long enough. It's time to grow up."

"I guess it is," he said.

"Then I can expect you back here by mid-afternoon?"

"Not under those conditions. I think I'll finish this circuit and decide then what I want to do with the rest of my life," he said.

"James Moses Crowe, you are a fool."

"Maybe, but it's my decision."

She slammed the phone down so hard that he held his ear for a moment.

He was still thinking about the conversation when he got to the farm. Jodie opened the back door of the rental and tossed her suitcases inside. "I've got a couple more things but I can get them. We're running a little late. You have trouble waking up?"

"A little," he admitted.

She was back in a moment with the rest of her things.

"That's more than you brought home," he said.

"So? My friend, Jimmy Crowe, travels with more and it doesn't weigh him down," she said with a brilliant smile.

"So today you aren't cranky?"

"Today I'm in a good mood."

"Well, I'm not. I'm grouchy," he said.

"Want to talk about it?" She held her breath. Was it last night's kiss?

"No, I do not."

"Then stew in your own juices. I'm in a lovely mood and no one can ruin my day," she said.

It lasted until they reached the airport. Everything went fine until they were cleared to board the plane. They were shown to their first class seats and were getting settled in when Deanna appeared in the doorway, a smile on her face and diamonds on her ears and fingers. She wore a powder blue suit with an ultra short skirt and fitted jacket, carried a coat to match. Her three-inch spike heels and leather handbag matched perfectly. Even the carry-on tote she had slung over her shoulder was powder blue and bore her initials in gold.

The flight attendant about fell all over himself helping her get the tote bag into the overhead compartment. He held her coat while she slid into the seat right beside Jimmy.

She patted Jimmy on the leg leaving her hand on his thigh a moment longer than necessary. "Hello, James, darlin'. Surprised to see me?"

Jodie was speechless. Jimmy's face registered pure

shock but maybe he knew she was coming and didn't know how to tell Jodie. He'd hardly spoken three words to her after he'd said he was grouchy and she'd let him have his space. Now she wished she'd pried everything out of him.

"Where are you going?" he asked.

Jodie realized in that moment that he hadn't known anything and was as stunned as she was. One thing was for sure—this was not a coincidence. It was a preplanned attack and Jodie didn't like it one bit.

"I'm on my way to New York to do some shopping. Just a little layover here in Dallas that didn't amount to much, one in Atlanta for an hour, and then I'm off to New York. You will have to entertain me in Atlanta. An hour will give us time to have a drink and catch up. I've missed you." She squeezed his thigh.

"Sorry," Jimmy said. "We'll have to hurry from one end of the concourse to the other to catch our plane."

"Well, then we'll simply have to make the most of the time we have, won't we? I might even change your mind by the time we get to Atlanta. How about if we just get off there and blow off the rest of the trip? I love shopping in the South. Maybe we could look at china patterns? You are going to propose soon, you know?" She smiled as sweetly as if she were discussing what wine they'd have with dessert.

"I don't think so," he said.

The flight attendant went through the motions as she

showed them what to do in case of an emergency. Jodie wondered if the situation she and Jimmy were in could be considered an emergency. Could she toss Deanna out on the tarmac and declare it an act of saving grace? Surely Jimmy wasn't really attracted to a conniving witch like that. But then maybe he was. He didn't seem affected by Jodie's kisses so maybe her alter ego sitting there in a baby blue suit that cost as much as a good Lowline heifer was what really appealed to him. Maybe he liked the way syrup dripped from her feminine little lips when she informed him that they were about to be engaged.

"Now where were we?" Deanna asked when the lady was finished showing them how to use their seats as flotation devices.

Jodie envisioned the blue suit soaking wet and Deanna's hair hanging limp in her face. Would Jimmy like her so much then?

"Oh, yes," she said. "We were discussing china patterns. I'm thinking maybe we should have it custom designed. Something embossed with a C in the middle and a D on one side with a J on the other. That would symbolize our union but let us remain true to our own identities, don't you think?"

"I think you better be joking, Deanna. I have not nor do I intend to propose to you," Jimmy said bluntly.

"Oh, don't be difficult," she snapped. "What do you intend to do, marry this bull riding thing that doesn't know if she's a woman or a man?"

Jodie had heard enough. She reached over and removed Deanna's hand from Jimmy's leg, holding it up in the air only a moment before she dropped it like so much dirty laundry. "I do believe you are trespassing on my property, darlin'," she said just as sugary sweet as she could manage.

Deanna slid her a 'go-to-hell' look that should have chilled her to the bone. "What makes you think it's your property?"

Jodie was amused. She'd get him out of this but he'd owe her big time. No more grouchy moods. "Because we got married yesterday. Didn't you get your invitation?"

Deanna turned pale and immediately checked for rings. "You are lyin'. Neither of you are wearing a ring."

"That's right. We're having our plain gold bands engraved. They won't be ready for a week or two," Jodie lied.

"Does your grandmother know about this?" Deanna turned on him. Her face turned from sticky sweet to mean and hateful in a split second.

"I'm twenty-six years old. In the state of Oklahoma the legal age without parental consent is twenty-one," Jimmy said.

"They'll crucify you. You better enroll in a college class called Poor 101 because you have no idea how to live like you are about to," she told him.

"Aren't you going to wish us happiness?" Jodie taunted.

"No, I'm going to wish you misery and hope that before the week is out he figures out what a mistake he's made. But rest assured it's over between us, darlin'. Bobby Jack is meeting me in New York. I'd hoped I could call him and tell him that I'd had a change of heart. But I will have a wedding and I will choose china patterns this week. You can be the groom of the century or you can take a back seat to Bobby Jack."

"Good luck," Jimmy said.

Deanna waved at the attendant. "Please seat me somewhere else. I can't bear to spend two hours with these abominable people. They nauseate me."

"But madam, there are no more first class seats. We have lots of room in coach but we're full in this section," he said.

She was on her feet and headed to the back of the plane in moments. "I'll ride coach before I sit here."

Jodie tried to pull her hand away before it went up in flames but Jimmy held it tightly.

"What brought all that on?" He grinned.

"Thought I'd get you out of a planned marriage. You can always go back there and tell her you've had a change of heart," she said.

"Then we aren't really married?" he teased. For the second time in his life Jodie had come to his rescue. He rather liked this time even better than the last.

"No, and you don't have to enroll in Poor 101," she said.

"Yes, I do. My expense account was shut down this morning. That's why I was in a grouchy mood. I'm not poor by any means but I won't have the kind of money I'm used to spending on trips."

"I thought the PBR was financing our trip," she said.

"I'm freelance. I've got contacts but not an expense account from any of them. I take it off my taxes at the end of the year and repay the corporation out of my earnings. So far I haven't had a year in the red but some of them have been slim. Did I tell you I finished the book while we were home?"

Home? Where did that come from? Great God, have I made up my mind and decided that square mile of dirt is home?

The word didn't get past Jodie but she decided to let it rest until she had time to think about it. "No, you didn't. I would have thought that would make you happy rather than grouchy."

"It was the telephone conversation I had with Cathy that made me cranky," he admitted. Sitting there, holding her hand in his, he wanted to tell her everything. He wanted to tell her that he had indeed found his home, that being able to write so well had proven it. But he didn't want to spoil the moment. He didn't want to lose hold on her just when he'd discovered his true feelings for the woman.

"What?" Jodie relaxed her arm and kept her hand in

his even though the touch was playing havoc with her thinking ability.

"It's a long story," he said.

"We've got two hours unless Miss Blue Ice comes back. I don't reckon she'd want to hear it."

"She probably already knows. I've got a feeling Cathy put her on this plane and she's got no intentions of going to New York. She was here to show me the difference in the two of you and what I'm throwing away if I don't go back to San Antonio right now," he said and then he told her the rest of the story.

When the plane landed Deanna appeared as if by magic by Jimmy's side before he could even stand up. "I have been on the phone with your mother and grandmother as well as Cathy. Turn your cell phone on because they are trying to call you. You better talk fast and furious because you are in big trouble."

Jodie stood up and stretched like a lazy panther, working the kinks from her neck where she'd fallen asleep after listening to Jimmy's tale. "I don't think so, honey. I'm the teacher at Poor 101 and I think he'll be a fantastic student."

"Go to hell," Deanna hissed and stomped off the plane.

"You don't have to come to my defense, you know. I really can take care of myself," he said.

"But it's so much fun. Especially after the way she baited me about bull riding and looked down on me.

I'm actually not taking up for you but getting a little revenge," Jodie said.

"So you are ten feet tall and bullet-proof?"

"Today I am. And let me tell you something, honey. If I thought for one minute you weren't man enough to take care of yourself, I wouldn't be traveling with you. You are a damn good writer and you'll make it fine on your own without anyone shoving money in your bank account. I don't keep company with wimps. Never have and don't plan on starting now. I'm hungry. Let's go find something fast and cheap."

Jimmy's heart swelled and his soul soared. She believed in him. Someone as tough and brassy as Jodie Cahill had just paid him the biggest compliment he'd ever had.

The first place they passed on their way to their next flight was Taco Bell. She declared she could eat a half dozen tacos and an order of beans. "So we're going to do the cheap hotels and bologna sandwiches when we get back to Florida?"

He picked up the tray with their orders and carried them to the nearest table. "Guess so."

"Hmmm, you think you'll get fat eating like that?"

"Tacos?"

"No, bologna sandwiches and Wal-Mart brand chips?"

"I might. You going to divorce me if I outgrow my britches?" he teased.

"No, I betcha there's still some bibbed overalls in

your grandpa's closet you could wear. When are you starting your next book?"

"Why do you ask?"

"Did you get a good advance on this one?"

"I thought so. If I lived at the ranch and was careful it might pay the bills for a year. That's saying that I didn't take a bull rider to dinner at fancy restaurants real often," he said.

"How many books could you write in a year if you had the time to stay with it?"

"Two, maybe three," he said.

"Do you enjoy writing novels or traveling around doing freelance work for newspapers and magazines?"

"I didn't realize it but I really liked staying at the old house these past few days and writing. I don't think my grandfather would appreciate that somehow. He didn't want my dad to be anything but a rancher. The picture in the box of mementos that Kay gave me was of me in jeans and a Western shirt. I think he got his mind set that the little boy in the picture would grow up to be a rancher like him, but I'm not."

"Your life is not about what your grandmother and mother want. It's also not about what Ratch wanted. It's your choice, Jimmy. My folks wanted me to go to college like my sisters. I hated it. What's that old saying . . ." she paused for a minute.

"To thine own self be true?" he asked.

"That's it," she said and went back to eating.

Chapter Fifteen

"Welcome to Dade City—Proud Heritage—Promising Future." Jodie read the brick rectangular sign as they drove into the town. "Dade City, population 6,188, my kind of town."

"Why is it your kind of town? And what's the name of the rodeo tonight?" Jimmy asked.

"It's the Pasco County Fair and Championship Rodeo. It's my kind of town because it's about the size of Sulphur. I like small towns where everyone knows what everyone else is doing and they only read the local weekly paper to see who got caught. We only spend one night here and then it's on to your kind of town. Davie is right next to Ft. Lauderdale. Big and impersonal.

Aha, there's a motel. Let's stop and, no, it's already got a NO VACANCY sign in the window."

"And what makes a big town my kind of town? Thank God we're not stopping there," Jimmy said.

"Why? Already squeamish about where you lay your little head at night? Tassels on your shoes and nutritious food makes it your kind of town."

He set his jaw and kept driving.

She pointed to the next motel on the highway. "Right there. Try that one."

He pulled in and she bailed out. In a few minutes she was back at the door she'd left wide open. "They've got one room left. Called all over town but everything is booked solid with the rodeo going on. You want it or do we drive all night after the rodeo is over?"

He handed her the credit card and hoped it had two beds. He'd rather drive all night than sleep on the floor of a motel where he could already hear the theme song from "The Twilight Zone" playing in his head. Or was that the music from *Psycho*? Or worse yet had orange shag carpet that smelled like forty years of dirty feet.

She came back with an old-fashioned key with a big chunk of plastic on the ring. The room number had been embossed in gold at one time. Now it was barely visible.

She stuck her head inside the truck and told him, "Number Twenty, all the way to the end," and then jogged down the length of the small motel.

He parked the truck right in front of the room where she'd already gone inside. By the time he unloaded a couple of suitcases and his laptop she was coming out of the bathroom. It wasn't the Hilton or the Hyatt Regency but it looked comfortable enough for one night.

"Which bed do you want?" she asked.

He looked at both of them. Twins in every way. Stiff bedspreads in a profusion of colorful swirls in some kind of material NASA considered using for the space program, guaranteed to hold its shape and color under a nuclear attack. The flat pillows didn't fare so well. Too many rodeo bronc riders had tumbled their big heads down on them. One bed was beside the heating unit under the window covered with matching drapes that bagged open in the middle and one on the side where the dressing area/bathroom was located.

"It doesn't matter."

"Then I'll take the one by the bathroom," she said.

They'd shared a trailer not much bigger but it did have a door between the bedroom and living area. There was very little size difference but that was before and now he didn't look forward to sleeping in a bed right beside hers.

But that could be a blessing, his conscience said. *If she talks in her sleep or snores or both I might find something I hate. Absolutely abhor to the point that I'll be glad to take her back to Cahill ranch and get rid of her in six weeks. This whole thing with keeping the ex-*

pense account down could be my salvation. Besides who's to say that she won't be a nice person at all when she doesn't have all the comforts of my high-end expense account?

She carried in one suitcase and a grocery bag of food they'd bought in the first grocery store she spotted after they left the airport.

He didn't think for one minute a change of venue was going to turn her into a shrew. She could probably sleep in a two-man pup tent with a shovel to use when necessity called and not complain.

"In forty-five minutes we've got to be at the rodeo arena. No time to eat until afterward so I'm having yogurt and a banana. We've got Pringles, peanut butter crackers, Club crackers, cheese in a can, and apples. You want something?" she asked.

He cut his eyes around at her. "You're eating healthy food?"

"There ain't no double bacon cheeseburgers in this bag, darlin'. I'm eating whatever will keep body and soul together until after the judging tonight. Then I'll find a place that serves something greasy."

There went his dimples, she thought. *How could I have ever thought those were wrinkles?*

"I'll pass. Maybe when we get back to the room tonight I'll make a smoothie," he said.

She wolfed down two containers of yogurt and a couple of bananas, then went to work in front of the mirror. He set up his computer and began to hunt medium-priced hotels in or near Davie for the next two nights. He completely lost track of time as he flipped from one place to the other seeing which was closest to the Bergeron rodeo grounds.

"Hey, how big is your pride?" she asked right behind him.

He stiffened to keep from jumping. "Too big. Why?"

"I've got an idea about the next six weeks but you're going to have to swallow some of that male ego of yours before I put it into play," she told him.

He closed the computer and stood up, really looking at her. She wore a new outfit, evidently one she'd gotten while they were in Sulphur. Tight black jeans with a hot pink Western-cut shirt and a lighter pink fringed leather jacket, fitted to the waist where a gold belt buckle gleamed. She held a hat the same color as her shirt with a band of gold filigree. His mind went completely blank. She'd asked him something about his pride but he couldn't remember what it was.

"So?" she asked.

"What?"

"You must have been enthralled by whatever you were looking up on that computer. I asked if we're a team yet?"

"No, you didn't. You said something about my ego and pride," he remembered.

"Well, are we a team? Are we friends?"

"Yes, to both."

"Okay, then, don't go getting all macho on me in the next ten minutes."

He looked at the alarm clock on the nightstand beside the bed. They had fifteen minutes before it was time to go. His face held a quizzical look when he looked back at her. She had a cell phone to her ear.

"Hello, Irene, this is Jodie Cahill. Is the man still in the office?"

Jimmy retrieved his jacket from a garment bag and listened at the same time.

"Hello. Yes, things are going fine but I've got an idea for the rest of the trip I'd like to run past you. You got the schedule right there in front of you, right?"

She waited a minute. "Okay, tomorrow night we need to be in Davie, Florida. You with me? What I want is motel rooms added in as part of my judging. You can give them a lower rate on my judging fee but I want a motel room in each town from now on. They'll be getting a deal because they can comp out the rooms through the local chamber in most cases and get my judging for half price, and I'll be getting a good deal because I won't have to look for a room in every town."

She listened again.

"It doesn't have to be five stars or even four but I don't want roaches or rats. The closer to the rodeo grounds the better in every case. Just get me a room with two beds, fridge, and microwave, if it's available, when we're in the same place for more than one night. Think you could take care of that for me?"

He couldn't believe she had that much clout. But then he realized the buckle she wore was the gold one she'd earned when she won the Nationals. That made her a bit of a celebrity.

"Thank you. No, I don't need the whole itinerary right now. Send it as Irene makes the plans to . . . just a minute"—she handed him the phone—"Tell Irene your email address."

He rattled off the address and gave the phone back to Jodie.

"Thanks a bunch, Irene. We'll check it before we leave in the morning. Anyone doesn't want to play by the new rules, threaten them." She laughed, asked about Irene's children and grandchildren and snapped the phone shut.

"What did that have to do with us being a team or friendship?" he asked.

She started for the door. "I was afraid you'd go all macho and declare your part of the deal was to pay expenses."

"You got a way to make a deal for gasoline?" he asked.

She grinned. "No, but I'm taking every mile off my taxes next year."

Though small, the rodeo wasn't any less exciting. The announcer introduced her as a past winner of the National Professional Bull Riding competition. She stood up and her belt buckle glittered under the lights. The crowd went crazy; applause and catcalls filled the arena. Jimmy wondered if the buckle was insured. Folks had been shot in the back for a lot less. He filed the thought in the back of his mind to ask about later.

The bull riders were in fine form and twice they had to call on the chute judge to break a tie. One rider was sent off to the hospital in the ambulance but before the evening ended the announcer let everyone know the young rider had only fractured his wrist. Jodie sympathized with him. His career for this year was most likely over and until he'd gotten hung up he had a really good score.

Jimmy packed his camera and notebook into the canvas tote bag he carried and went to the judges' stand after the last ride was finished. She greeted him with a smile and declared she was hungry enough to eat a rear haunch off a bucking bull.

"And honey, that part of the expense account is still on you," she said.

That had to be three or four times she'd called him by that endearment that day. He wasn't sure if he liked it or if he wanted her to stop.

"Well, they've already put the bulls away for the evening so what else could you eat?"

She kept pace beside him, her long legs matching his stride, step for step. They were a team, friends like she said. But suddenly, as he walked beside her in her pink cowgirl get-up, he wanted more than that. He didn't want to get over her as Paul told him to do; he didn't care what anyone else thought of her, including Cathy.

"I've thought about it. I saw a Captain D's on the way to the motel. I could go for some fish and chips. But I'd like to take it back to the room. I'd cry if I got grease all over this jacket. I just got it out of the cleaners a couple of months ago," she said.

"Then Captain D's it is. Is that fast food?"

A grin stretched her full mouth out to the fullest. "You bet it is. Fried fish, fried potatoes, corn on the cob, hush puppies. Aren't your little fat cells just wiggling in anticipation?"

"They're wearing black in preparation for a cholesterol funeral," he said.

At the drive-by window they ordered the dinner for four with her swearing the whole time that they should get the one for six. They took it back to the motel and she hurriedly flipped through a topsy-turvy suitcase, grabbed a couple of items, and disappeared into the bathroom. He heard the shower running and a single swear word when she bumped her elbow on the door as she got dressed. He put on a pair of pale blue cotton pajamas and a white tank top. Then he set about putting the food on a little round table with two chairs pushed up in the corner beside the heating unit.

He bit back a smile when she came out dressed in a nightshirt with the Tasmanian Devil on the front and a pair of faded boxer shorts. An hour ago she was the queen of Pasco County. Now she looked like the queen of a double wide.

"What are you grinning about?" she asked.

"Taz. He fits you," he said.

She sat down at the table and started eating. "Probably so. I can be a real devil when I'm hungry. You'd better sit down and lay claim to part of this if you don't want to starve to death. If your stomach wakes me up growlin' in the night, I'm going to kick you out in the yard."

He grabbed a piece of fish. Actually he'd planned on having yogurt and fruit. Heavy food at eleven o'clock at night wasn't healthy but he wasn't going to argue with her. He didn't doubt for one minute she'd try to kick him out. There'd be a brawl and he'd probably lose half the money his father left him paying the court costs and remodeling a motel built in the late 60's, but he'd give her a run for her money if push came to shove. The image of the two of them wrestling around, tearing up the motel room, and then spending time in court was enough to make him grin.

Hey, there's a new idea for a book. Husband and new wife get into a scrap in a cheap motel. The next day she's found dead in a bar ditch. Who killed her?

"What are you thinking about?" she asked between bites.

"Why?"

"You got this look on your face I've never seen before," she told him.

He opened his canvas bag and took out a small spiral notebook. "I was thinking about a new book idea. I need to write it down before I forget it."

"Just like that? Was it about fish and chips?" she asked.

He wrote a few lines and put the book back. "No. You really want to know?"

"Yes, I do."

"You said you'd kick me out in the yard if my stomach growled and woke you up." He went on to tell her the whole thing.

"Good Lord, you got an idea like that from a single sentence. You really are a writer. Can you produce a book from that?"

"Sure. I'll research a few weeks and then start writing. I won't even need to go on a three-month tour of bull riding to do it," he said.

"I'm impressed, but you better eat more than one piece of fish. I really will start kicking if you wake me up. Come to think of it, why don't I just go ahead and do it? Then you'll have firsthand experience to write about. I bet we could destroy this room in an hour if we really got into it."

"No thank you. Push those hush puppies over here. I don't want to lose a dime of my inheritance. I've got it dog-eared for something else," he said.

"What's that?"

"Part of it to remodel that house I just inherited.

God, that sofa in the living room is ugly and the springs are popping up in two of the cushions. And the whole place needs painting. And those ducks have got to go. They give me the hives. I'm going to make an office out of my old room and take Grandpa's for my bedroom. It's big enough to put a queen-sized bed in," he said.

She didn't know whether to laugh or cry. To have him that close would mean she could pursue him on a higher level than friendship, but if he wasn't interested, it would be a heartbreaker.

"Why queen-sized?" she asked.

"Full size is too short for tall folks like me. You should know that as tall as you are. Someday I plan to have a wife, Jodie. And I don't want a king-sized bed. Queen sized is long enough so my feet don't hang off the end but narrow enough to allow cuddling."

She almost choked on a sip of Dr. Pepper. She could see herself wrapped up in his arms, her head laid on that broad expanse of chest with soft blond curly hair tickling her cheek.

"Your turn."

She swallowed hard. He'd told her the truth and she'd be honor-bound to do the same, yet the idea of voicing aloud the thoughts she'd just had made her blush. "My turn?" She tried to buy a little time.

He pushed the paper container of fish across the table. "Yeah, your turn. I've had two slabs of fish while you were sitting there daydreaming."

She picked up a piece and shoved half of it in her mouth.

"Jodie, do you really really think I'd be happy in Sulphur just living out there on my grandpa's ranch and writing?"

She swallowed, grateful that he hadn't asked what she was daydreaming about. "It's your ranch, not your grandpa's. And only you can answer that. Nothing says you can't try it. If you hate the place after a few months, sell it and go back to the city. Nothing ventured, nothing gained."

"Sounds like good advice. Now on to the next big item. It's a five-hour drive from here to Davie. Checkout is eleven so we shouldn't be pressed too much for time. I'm wired and need to write. You want to sleep and take the first shift at driving tomorrow?"

"Sure thing. Let me clean off this table. You set up your computer and see if there's an email yet so we'll know where we're stayin' tomorrow night."

She was brushing her teeth when he yelled across the room and over the sound of the running water to tell her they'd be staying at the LaQuinta Inn and there was a shuttle from the hotel to the rodeo grounds.

"That sounds just fine," she said around a mouth full of toothpaste.

She threw back the covers on the bed she'd chosen and stretched out. He was right. Unless she drew her knees up the bed was way too short. He had his back to her, the width of his shoulders stretching the gauzy fabric of the tank top. Didn't the man have a flaw? She finally flipped over and shut her eyes but the mental picture stayed with her a long time before she finally drifted off to sleep to dream of riding the bull again—the one that caused her death.

She awoke in a sweat, unfamiliar with her surroundings and terrified. For a brief moment she thought she'd really died. The room was so dark, then something crawled across her cheek and brought her back into reality with a start. She felt her face and the creepy critter crawled right onto her hand. She slung it at the wall and screamed, shivering from her head to her toes, suddenly standing in the middle of the bed doing something akin to break dancing as she fought with other imaginary bugs.

Jimmy came out of a deep sleep with a start and jumped out of bed, stubbed his toe on one of her pink boots and fell across her bed, his eyes wide as he tried to put things in focus. "What in the hell is going on?" he asked.

"Bug," she yelled.

"Where?" He squinted in the darkness.

"Over there. It's big and hairy and it was on my face," she said.

He fumbled from the bed to the light switch and bathed the room in light.

She went into more spasms, jerking around in a

haze before him. "Oh, my God, it's a cockroach and it touched me."

"Just a minute, Jodie. I can't see a thing. Give me a minute to put my contacts in, and I'll take care of it." He made his way to the vanity and his stomach growled. Was that what set this fit off? Was she getting geared up to try to kick him outside?

She picked up a boot and chased the roach around the baseboards, finally cornering it not a foot from where he stood. A brown residue was all that was left on the wall when she stopped beating it to death. "They can repaint the place and use a little bug spray while they're at it," she said. "I hate roaches. For a minute, I thought the dang thing was a spider and I hate them even worse."

"Well, we are good and awake now," he said grumpily. "I've had all of," he looked at the clock, "good grief, it's fifteen minutes until eleven. The alarm didn't work. I set it for ten."

"And you pinned the drapes together too, didn't you?"

"Yes, I did. I didn't want daylight waking us up."

"Well, I guess we'd better bless the roach and get our things together."

So he was blind as a bat without contacts. That could be a flaw but then in another avenue of thought, it could be a blessing. It might be nice knowing he couldn't focus on her the first thing in the morning when she was wrinkled and gray-haired.

Chapter Sixteen

March came in like a roaring lion. Jodie and Jimmy were on an forty-mile stretch of Texas 288 South when the storm hit, blowing rain in sheets so thick and dark that visibility was scarcely two yellow lines on the highway. Jimmy's knuckles turned white around the steering wheel as he crept along, cars in front of him, semis passing on the left, a van behind him. He could see little and hear even less with the force of the storm showing no signs of letting up.

They'd just finished two days in Davie, Florida, drove almost twelve hundred miles to Houston where they worked the Rodeo Houston for three nights, and were on their way to Bay City for three nights. Weariness was setting into Jimmy's bones. True, he was getting the feel of what real rodeo followers endured, but he was ready to go home and right that minute he didn't even care where home was.

Jodie was so restless she had trouble sitting still in the passenger's seat and it had nothing to do with the storm. Jimmy was a capable driver, and she trusted him not only with her vehicle but her life. It was the latter that caused the agitation. Sure, she believed he'd take care of her in an emergency, but could she or rather *would* she trust him with her heart? Not that he'd made any kind of overtures in the past week. They'd settled into a comfortable routine. Judge a rodeo. Either eat with friends or take food back to the room afterwards. Jimmy wrote half the night and they both slept late. Old friends or roommates sharing a journey and a hotel room, but nothing more.

"What's the next exit and how far?" he asked.

She brushed his arm when she leaned across him to get a better view of the odometer. The sensation it caused wasn't a surprise but it always made her gasp. "Five miles and it's a right hand exit onto Texas Highway 35. From there it's about thirty-six miles into Bay City. They've got us a room at the Econolodge, which is less than three miles from the arena. Maybe this will blow through by then."

"Don't imagine they have valet parking, do they?" he asked wistfully.

"No, but they usually have a carport and there's an umbrella back there," she said.

"Are you being snippy with me? I can pull this thing off to the side and you can drive if you're going to be hateful."

"I'm not being snippy or hateful. Don't take it out on me because you're on edge."

"I don't like it when you act like that, Jodie."

"Like what?"

"You know what I'm talking about. Tassels on my shoes. Big cities. It's like you're talking down to me because I'm different than you are."

She chewed on that for several minutes. He was different but then so was she. Perhaps that was the gulf between them, preventing the physical attraction from becoming something more. At least he didn't call her a country hick or a redneck so what right did she have to tease him about his preferences? She couldn't find an answer to come back with so she meditated a little longer.

"I'm fighting against my heart," she said finally. "If I keep finding things wrong with you then I can tell it that I really don't like you."

It was his turn to digest what she'd just admitted and it scared the bejesus out of him. Her honesty had stunned him from the beginning and in the seven weeks they'd shared lives it still amazed him that a woman could just say what was on her mind. Most of the females in his world were cloying at the very least. Not Jodie Cahill. She spoke her mind and if Jimmy wanted an answer or the truth, all he had to do was ask the question.

"You going to say anything?" she asked.

"I think I might. Give me a minute to get my ducks in a row," he answered.

"Take all the time you need, but there's the exit. You're already in the right lane so just slow down and ease off on the ramp," she said.

"I don't need you to tell me how to drive," he quipped.

Lightning joined the rain and streaked across the darkness in zig-zags that brought on rolling thunder. It was so loud that Jodie covered her ears with her hands like a child.

"You think we should pull over at that service station until this passes?" she asked.

"No, we'll keep on. Maybe we'll outrun it," he said. He caught Texas 35 and started the southwest drive into Bay City.

"You got them ducks in a row yet?" she asked.

"Okay, but don't get mad," he said.

Her heart turned to stone and dropped out the floorboard of the truck onto the wet pavement. The pain was such that she figured he'd already crushed it with the back wheels.

"I knew you before I asked if you'd accompany me on the rounds. I was in your kindergarten class and I was there on that rodeo day your folks had for the class," he said.

Her heart leaped back into her chest. She'd expected

him to say that he could never be interested in a rancher for anything but a friend or, worse yet, the old cliché about feeling like she was his sister. She would have cried right there in front of him if he'd said that.

"Do you remember what happened that day?" he asked.

"No, that was a long time ago. I guess we had some sheep for the kids to ride and maybe a pony. Why?"

"It wouldn't have been a big deal to you but it was to me," he said.

"Because?" She waited.

"Because it was the second day of school. Because I wore these thick eyeglasses and was a skinny little kid with no friends since we moved all the time. Anyway, the first day of school you were the only one who said hello to me or offered to let me play with your group. That would be Stella, Rosy, and Dee. The next day was the rodeo at your folks' ranch. My dad and mom fought that morning. He said he'd gone into town and bought me the jeans and shirt so I'd look like the other kids. She said her child wasn't wearing that kind of clothes because we weren't staying on the ranch. Finally, she let him win, and I wore the jeans. Do you remember anything about the day?"

"No, Jimmy, I don't. I know that your dad was dying by the time you got back home but that's only because you told me."

"There was a big kid. I can't even remember his name but he was the biggest boy in class and he was a bully deluxe."

"Joel Curtis," she remembered out of the rainy sky.

"That's right. I'd forgotten his name. I was sitting all by myself on a bale of hay, just watching the other kids participate in a race. Anyway, he yelled at me and called me Four Eyes and then told me I was a sissy because I played with girls. Then he drew back and popped me right in the face. Bloodied my nose. I lost my glasses and couldn't see him so there I was holding my nose, blind and scared to death plus mortified."

"He's still egotistical. And I'm beginning to remember that day. I didn't know it was you he'd been mean to that day. We were enemies from then on. He tried to put a wedge between me and Stella. Dated her in high school. I told her he was bad news."

The rain turned into a drizzle. The sky was still gray but ahead the clouds were less ominous, and a ray or two of sunshine could be seen.

"You came running over there and found my glasses for me, then you literally took him to the ground. I thought you'd kill him you were hitting him so hard, and he was crying and carrying on worse than me by the time some mothers came and pulled you off him," Jimmy said.

"The reason I don't remember is that it wasn't the only time I whooped Joel Curtis. That just must have been the first time he made me mad." She wondered what Joel and a child's fight had to do with her just declaring that she might like Jimmy.

"Well, it was the only time something like that happened to me. Add that in to going home to find my father about dead and then being jerked back into another lifestyle all in one day. And at five years old."

"Whew! Some bad day, wasn't it?"

"And the only bright spot in the whole thing was Jodie Cahill because she came to my rescue. I buried you deep in my heart and set you up on a pedestal so high even the angels couldn't see you."

She blushed scarlet.

"I made you out to be the perfect woman through the years. I measured everyone I dated by the Jodie Cahill yardstick. Would they walk right up to me and take me to their playgroup even though I was the new skinny kid who wore thick glasses and was so shy and backward I stuttered? Would they fight for me? Needless to say, no one measured up."

"I'm sorry," she said.

"Don't be," he said.

The rain lessened as they drove through it. He switched the windshield wipers from as fast as they could sweep to intermediate action. A road sign let them know they were only twenty miles from Bay City.

"Anyway to go on, I finally admitted my obsession to Paul. His grandparents liked television rodeo and while he was out there he heard about this new girl who was brave enough to ride bulls. We followed your career from then on. I got to know Sawyer and he kept me posted on what you were doing. Then one day he called and said he was bummed because he couldn't go on the rounds with you. You know the rest."

"You stalked me?" she asked.

"I guess I did."

"I'm not sure I like that. Have you gotten over this crazy infatuation with a person who's just a figment of your imagination?"

"I got over the infatuation. I keep telling Paul that but he doesn't believe me."

"Oh, so that's why Paul is your therapist? It's got to do with your obsession."

"Yes, it does. Like I said I'm over the infatuation."

She didn't know whether to demand that he stop the truck and let her walk the rest of the way to Bay City in the rain or to kick him out.

"But I'm not over you," he whispered.

"What?" She narrowed her eyes.

"From the beginning I've been on this trip to get over you. It didn't work. I'm fighting the same battle you are. With my heart. It knows I'm trying to find things, any-thing, to dislike and I keep failing and it keeps winning."

She was struck mute. So much explanation to get to such an abrupt ending. It was enough to boggle her poor little brain.

The rain completely stopped and a beautiful rainbow stretched across the sky. Brilliant reds, yellows, purples, blues all in an arch so perfect that it practically yelled about a pot of gold waiting at the end with a perky little leprechaun sitting on the side.

"So now you know. Are you angry or just grumpy?"

"Neither," she said. "Stunned is more like it."

"So what are we going to do about this? I really do like you, Jodie, but we are as different as night and day. You and your cowboy boots. Me with tassels on my expensive leather shoes."

"You bought boots, and I wore high heels to dinner at your folks," she reminded him.

"Yes, and we were both uncomfortable in those situations."

"Guess we don't have any choice about what to do for the next four weeks. We've got thousands of miles to travel. Hotels to stay in. Rides to judge. Articles to write. I suppose we are blessed. We've got a month to see if we can get along knowing that we like each other."

"Cursed is more like it. A month to live together and not do a thing about it. No more kisses either. Not when we've admitted this much and will be in such close proximity all these weeks," he groaned.

"There's the exit ramp for Bay City," she pointed. "I didn't say I was in love with you, James Moses Crowe. I said I liked you and honey, that's a big thing. It'll take more than four weeks for me to decide to move it up a tiny notch up the mile-high ladder. Love is all the way to the top. I've still got one foot on the ground, so you do the math."

A grin split his face as he nodded. They'd been together two months and look how far things had gone with them fighting it every step of the way. There was no telling what might happen in the next four weeks.

The smile disappeared. He shivered. Lord, what would happen if they did make it to the top of the ladder? A future with no end with Jodie Cahill? It was both exhilarating because life would be exciting every step of the way with her, and terrifying at the same time. Could he live in Murray County? Would she move to San Antonio?

Tingles slithered through Jodie's veins as she envisioned that ladder. True, she had one foot on the ground, but it was already begging to be allowed to climb up the ladder. The qualities that she hadn't liked in Jimmy from the beginning were fading and the ones she did admire were forcing themselves to the front. Like little children screaming and jumping up and down, vying for attention.

Suddenly the tassels on his shoes weren't any big thing. That he wore pleated slacks and silk shirts wasn't unappealing. When she shut her eyes to kiss him all those things disappeared anyway and all she saw was Jimmy Crowe, the man with a wonderful heart and soul.

Four weeks would be pure torture. They'd either kill each other or surely fall in love. In their world there seemed to be no gray matter, only pure black as in murder in the first degree or white, as in wedding dresses.

She stiffened her back to keep him from seeing the shiver. Lord, Almighty, she wasn't ready for that march down the aisle. She had to buy a ranch, prove that she could take care of herself, a million things before she consented to spend the rest of her life with one man.

Chapter Seventeen

True to Mother Nature's promise, March went out like a lamb. Almost anti-climactic, Jodie thought, as she drove her truck into the yard. In the past four weeks, since that horrible rainstorm when they were headed to Bay City, Texas, they'd traveled to Montgomery, Alabama, for three days; on to Arcadia, Florida, for three more; and then back to Austin, Texas, for a four-day stint before they were off to Fargo, Indiana, for a PRCA Championship Rodeo. Then it was a lazy four-day trip back to Nacogdoches, Texas. From there they went to Lubbock, Texas, and finally just the past two nights she'd judged the Texoma Livestock Show and Rodeo in Sherman, Texas.

If Jimmy was half as tired as she was, he was feeling

every aching bone in his body and yearning for hours and hours of rest. According to the speedometer and her mileage chart they'd traveled almost fourteen thousand miles in the past three months.

The lights were out in the house when she turned off the ignition and she was glad. As much as she'd missed her parents this last month, she wasn't ready to talk to anyone. Not until she had everything straightened out in her heart, which hopefully she would do after a good night's sleep. One night in her own bed surrounded by familiarity and she'd see things in a much different light, she was sure of it.

Jimmy began to unload his gear while she went inside and opened the garage door so he could get to his Mustang. He backed it out and tossed things haphazardly from the truck to the Mustang's back seat and trunk.

"So where are we?" he asked.

"Home," she said.

"You know what I mean, Jodie."

"Yes, I do, and I don't know. You planning on staying at the ranch a few days?" From Bay City on they'd skirted around the issue, not killing it outright but leaving it alive for future reference. Future was here and she still didn't know where they were.

"Right now I am. Mother and Grandmother are having a fit about it. Cathy has called several times to gripe and threaten me because I'm breaking my mother's heart. According to her, Mother worked her whole life just to get me away from such squalor, and now I'm falling right back into it."

"How do you feel?"

"I don't know. I'm too tired to think. I love my family. I do. But I'm not a puppet on a string to dance when they tell me and be put away when they want. I just need weeks and weeks of peace and quiet to sort things out."

"Me, too. So good night, Jimmy," she said.

"Good night." He got into his car and was gone before she retrieved the first of her baggage from the truck.

Once things were unloaded into the living room, she sat down on the sofa without turning on a light. All month she'd looked forward to the time when she'd be back home so she could think straight. Each morning she awoke and counted off another day, telling herself that there was no way she could be objective with him so close all the time. Granny Etta used to say that a woman could get used to hanging if she hung long enough. Jodie figured it was the fact they were together twenty-four hours a day, seven days a week that kept feeding the attraction. If she starved it for a few weeks, it might die in its tracks. Like the mean dog she'd heard about once. It would come to the backyard and growl and the woman of the home would throw food out, thinking that if the ugly dog was full it would go away. Finally, she figured out she was doing things wrong. If she didn't feed it, the dog would go away. So perhaps if she stopped feeding the attraction to Jimmy, it would simply disappear.

Getting home and having some space between them was what she needed. That and time. After a few months she'd look back and laugh about the trip with its ups and downs—heavy on the latter, please, ma'am.

She inhaled deeply and climbed the stairs to her room where she shucked out of jeans, a rhinestone-studded shirt, underwear, and a belt buckle that glittered in the lights of the opening ceremonies. She ran a deep, warm bath and settled into a mound of bubbles with a sigh. She leaned her head back and shut her eyes and fell asleep only to awaken shivering. The water had gone cold and the bubbles flat. A quick toweling off and she was off to bed, only to have her eyes spring open and refuse to shut.

Jimmy parked the car beside the front porch and fumbled with the unfamiliar lock on the door a full two minutes before he finally got inside the house. It was cold and musty again. He flipped on the living room lights and went straight to the wall thermostat, adjusted the heat and stumbled down the hall to his room. Thank goodness his grandparents had put in electric heat and air and he didn't have to light the fireplace and wait for warmth.

He fell back on the bed, fully dressed without even taking off his shoes, and shut his eyes. He'd thought the month would never end. Every night when Jodie went to bed he wanted to kiss her goodnight. Every morning he fought the urge to hug her and tell her that he had fallen in love with her. Every minute he reminded himself that although he had a few dollars in the bank and a nice portfolio from his investments from his inheritance from his grandfather, he did not have stability. Before he could offer her his heart he had to have a steady job. Freelance writing wasn't dependable enough, not in his eyes.

He was glad to be home. Glad to have time and space away from her so he could think rationally. Paul told him repeatedly that all girls looked like angels when you were floating in the clouds and had advised him to either come home or spend several weeks in a place where he couldn't see Jodie. See if the old adage about being out of sight, out of mind wouldn't prove true. Maybe it would, but he didn't think so. The trip to Oklahoma back in January had changed his life and way of thinking. Who would have thought a city boy could find such contentment sharing time and space with a rancher, and in an old frame house on a dirt farm?

Tree frogs and crickets made a mournful noise outside his window. Spring had sprung in the past three months and was about to take its rightful place by pushing winter into the history books. Jimmy rolled over and pulled the drapes back. A full moon lit up the yard like dim daylight. A black and white cat moved a litter of kittens one at a time from somewhere in the front yard—Jimmy guessed under the porch—toward the barn. Five of them—bundles she was protecting from him.

Finally he stood up and removed his shoes (with tassels on them), his slacks and shirt, and slipped into a pair of pajama bottoms. Without a shower or turning back the covers he picked up a hand-crocheted afghan he must've liked as a child because it was still across the foot of his bed, wrapped it around his body and laid down to sleep.

It didn't happen. He tossed and turned, looking several times off to his right to see if Jodie was sleeping in the bed beside him, the one that wasn't there. The one night of his life when he was finally alone and she still kept him awake. Something wasn't fair or right in that scenario. He'd just spent months of wishing and aching for time away from her so he could analyze his feelings and what did he do but miss her.

Jodie couldn't take another minute of the restlessness. It had to be settled and it had to be done that night. No more soft-shoe dancing around things. He could own up to feeling the same way she did or break her heart. Either would be better than the hollow emptiness in her heart.

The bright red numbers on the digital clock beside her bed said it was two-thirty A.M. when she slipped on a pair of gray sweat pants and a flannel work shirt. Fear almost drove her back into the house when she turned the key to start the truck, but she shook it off. He might tell her that he hated the area the minute he walked back inside Ratch's house, but knowing was better than not knowing. Sleeping with a broken heart would be better than not sleeping at all.

Jimmy saw the lights in the driveway and checked the clock. Who on Earth would be coming to an old farm-house at this time of the morning? His first thought was that his mother and grandmother, who both knew he'd be going home tonight, had sent Paul or Cathy or a combination of his friends to influence him to come back to Texas. He set his jaw in anger. He was a grown man and had told them all he could make his own decision. He stomped up the hallway and slung open the door just as Jodie started to knock.

"Jodie?" He was amazed to see her standing there.

"Who were you expecting?" she snapped. Good grief, had he called Deanna or another woman? Had he made up his mind to forget all about her and moved on already?

"Certainly not you at this time of the morning. Is something wrong?"

"Yes, it is," she said. "Are you going to invite me in, or is there someone in there already?"

"Yes, I mean no. Yes, come inside. No, there's not anyone in here," he stammered.

"God, that sofa is ugly," she laughed nervously when she walked through the front door into the living room.

"It's getting replaced first thing tomorrow morning. You know a good furniture store?"

"Rick's in Sulphur or you could go to Ardmore where there's a bigger selection, but I bet Rick would have something you'd like," she said. *Why are we talking about a sofa when there was so much to be said?*

"What time do they open?" he asked.

"Nine, I guess."

"Want to go furniture shopping with me? I'm thinking about a queen-sized bedroom suite and a new refrigerator and stove too."

"Love to," she said.

"Is that what you came out here for? To tell me the sofa was ugly?" he asked.

Her courage faltered and she headed toward the door. "I guess it is. Now that I've made you aware of that bit of bad news, I'm going home."

In the time it takes a gnat to blink he grabbed her arm and swung her around. In the next microsecond his lips found hers and the whole last month faded into a blur. Destiny fulfilled its course in life as heartbeat met heartbeat and they admitted they were in love without saying a word.

He broke away but kept her in his arms, inhaling the sweet smell of shampoo in her long brown hair. "I love you, Jodie Cahill. I don't have a thing to offer you except a ranch that hasn't seen any improvements in twenty years, a barn full of equipment that's so old it might not even start, and an ugly sofa."

She leaned back and looked into those dark green eyes. "Are you proposing to me?"

He nodded. "I am but you won't be getting much except a man who's been in love with you for more than twenty years."

"Yes, I will marry you, James Moses Crowe. I love you too. I came out here to tell you that if you wanted to go back to San Antonio, I'd sell my livestock and go with you if you'd have me."

"You'd do that for me?"

"Honey, I'd follow you to the end of the world."

"Tonight I feel like we've been there and back. What time does the courthouse open? Think we could get married and get a sofa the same day?"

She laughed. "We're having a wedding. Not a big one. Just something with friends and family. Maybe at the lodge. Call your mother and grandmother and Cathy. Tell them they will be guests at the lodge for the weekend. Tell Cathy we'll put her on the ground floor."

"Do I have to?" he asked.

She nodded. "You got to make peace with them someday. Might as well start off on a clean slate with our marriage."

"I guess if you'd be willing to go to the ends of the earth I can make one call," he promised and kissed her again.

The wedding was held two weeks later at the lodge. Jodie wore a white cotton dress with her white cowboy boots. Instead of a veil she chose a new white felt hat with a hatband of illusion caught up in a bow at the back and satin streamers down her back. A bouquet of multi-colored wild flowers lay across one arm while the other was looped through her father's as they descended the staircase together.

Jimmy wore a black Italian suit with a boxy jacket, a white silk shirt, black tie, and shoes with tassels on them.

Roseanna served as maid of honor. Paul stood beside Jimmy as his best man. The house overflowed with family and friends but from the time Jimmy looked into Jodie's eyes, there was no one within a hundred miles but the two of them. They said their vows and he placed the gold wedding band on her finger.

"And now you may kiss your bride," the preacher said. And he did.

"If that's any indication of how long this marriage will last, I think we'll see one of those eternal things," Roxie said to Jimmy's grandmother.

"Too bad," Cathy said just loud enough for Roxie to hear.

Roxie leaned down and whispered in her ear. "Young lady, you need a month in Murray County to adjust your attitude."

"Forty-eight hours in this godforsaken place is forty-seven too many," she shot right back.

"Then you go home to Texas but if you cause a bit of trouble between our new married couple you will answer to me, and I don't care what physical condition you're in. I'll kick your tail all the way across these United States and enjoy doing it."

Before Cathy could say a word, Roxie was headed toward the front of the lodge to kiss the groom and give her best congratulatory hug to the bride.

"How long do we have to stay?" Jimmy whispered out of the corner of his mouth as he graciously shook hands and received hugs.

"Not long," Jodie answered back.

Cathy rolled her wheelchair to the front of the lobby and extended her hand to Jodie. "You will let him come to San Antonio to see us occasionally?"

Jimmy stooped to hug her. "Does that include an invitation for Jodie as well?"

"Of course not. We'd like some time with you alone," Cathy said.

Jimmy stood up. "For the first few years you'll simply have to make time to come see us. We're going to be busy trying to make a ranch pay for itself and I'm already outlining a new mystery."

Melanie, Jodie's older sister, brought a man over to the wheelchair. "Oh, Cathy, I want you to meet my brother-in-law. My husband is Jim and this is his brother, Kent, who is a physical therapist when he's not busy running an oil company. I know you two will have a lot to talk about."

Kent shook hands with Cathy and then without asking took the handles of the wheelchair and escorted her out onto the deck.

"Hmmm," Jodie grinned.

"Poor Kent," Jimmy chuckled.

It was two hours later when Jodie and Jimmy finally left the reception in a flurry of rice showering down on their heads. The sky looked like someone had spilled yellow, orange, pink, and burgundy paint in a wide splash as the sun set that evening. Jodie leaned across the console in the Mustang and kissed Jimmy on the cheek.

"When we get really rich I want an old 1952 Chevrolet," she said.

"Why?"

"Because they have bench seats and really wide back seats," she said.

"Aha, my wife thinks we'll be young forever. Did I tell you that you are absolutely beautiful tonight? Did I tell you I'm the luckiest man in the world? That I'm glad what I hoped to accomplish didn't come true?"

"Fifty-two times but I'll never get tired of hearing

that. Did I tell you that you aren't what I hoped to marry?"

His face fell, and she giggled. "You aren't my darlin'. You are so much more than my hopes could have imagined."

"Sit right there," he said when he stopped the car in front of the ranch house.

He ran around the car and opened the door but before she could step out he scooped her up into his arms and carried her across the yard and the porch. He'd purposely left the door unlocked so it would be easy to open.

He set her down in the living room where a dozen candles flickered and roses were strewn in a pathway leading from the front door to the queen-sized bed awaiting them. He removed her cowboy hat and sent it sailing to the new sofa, made of a soft brown leather that invited them to snuggle down together at the end of a long day. "Welcome home, Mrs. Jodie Crowe."

She tangled her fingers in those soft blond curls on his shirt collar and pulled his face toward hers. "Welcome home to you, James Moses Crowe," she said just before her lips found his.

He scooped her up again, pushed a button on a CD player and Rascal Flatts began to sing their song, "Bless the Broken Road." By the time he laid her ever so gently on a bed scattered with red rose petals, the singer talked about seeing how *every sign pointed straight to you* and *every long lost dream lead me to where you are.*

He removed her cowboy boots. "It's true, isn't it? The broken road brought me home to you. Do you believe in fairy tales?"

"And they lived happily ever after," she whispered.

Epilogue

7 years later

Jodie wasn't ready for her son, Ratch, to go to kinder-garten. The first day hadn't been easy for her even if he did tell her he was a big boy and ready to go off to school. He was all excited about seeing his friends every day: Stella and Rance's oldest son, Justin; Dee and Jack's second child, Forrest; Greta and Kyle's prissy daughter, Emalee; Rosy and Trey's twins, Van and Marie. He was elated and didn't even see her wipe away tears as she left him in care of the teacher.

The next day was rodeo day at the Crowe ranch so Jodie didn't have a problem with tears that day. The whole kindergarten class brought their lunch in paper bags and wore their favorite Western clothes. Ratch wore a rodeo clown outfit. He'd been mutton busting and clowning for two years already and her heart swelled as she helped him put on his baggy pants and painted his face.

Jimmy leaned against the door jamb and watched them getting ready for the big day. That's all he'd heard about for a week. All of Ratch's friends were coming and anyone who wanted to could ride the sheep. He'd teach them all about mutton busting and how to hang on for the full eight seconds. He was even going to share his bull-on-a-limb with whoever wanted to ride it. Jodie's father had given him his favorite toy when he was three years old. An old tractor tire had been cut into the shape of a bull and hung on four ropes from a sturdy tree limb. Ratch had won the gold buckle a hundred times and that poor old tire bull had had the devil kicked out of him almost every day, winter and summer alike.

Jimmy had sold two books a year and it had kept them afloat there at first but in the last two years, Jodie had made the ranch pay for itself. Her Lowline cattle herd was growing and she had a rule. If it wasn't raised on Crowe ranch it wasn't used on Crowe ranch. That went for most of their food as well as what she raised for cattle.

He'd wanted to build a new home but she wouldn't have any part of that idea. She did consent to add a wing to the house to give them a bigger living room and a couple of extra bedrooms to house the growing Crowe family. Three kids in seven years and another on the way.

"So you about ready, Mr. Rodeo Clown?" Jimmy asked.

Ratch adjusted his glasses and winked. "Yes, I am. Turn them muttons loose and I'll show everybody how to tame 'em."

"Daddy, how do I look?" Their four-year-old daughter, Novaline, pranced into the room in designer jeans and a T-shirt with a crown made of rhinestones on the front. She wore pink cowboy boots to match her shirt and carried a hat of the same color.

"You look beautiful, Princess, but remember you only get to go to this because you live here. It's really a party for your brother's class," Jimmy reminded her.

"I know but next year I get to go to school and it will be my rodeo day because Momma said so, and I'm going to show them all how to barrel race on my pony," she said.

He hugged her. "You can do that sweetheart. I hear the bus. Jodie, I'll get the baby in the stroller."

"That would be wonderful. Bring her out to the corral. That's where the games will be all morning," Jodie said.

Jimmy found Kyle, Trey, Jack, and Rance all leaning against the corral fence post. Kids were running every which way as the mothers and teachers gave them free rein before organized games started.

Trey and Jimmy looked as out of place as chicken droppings on a birthday cake in dress slacks and three-button polo shirts, but they were just as interested in their little ranch hands as the rest of the family.

"So has Rosy entered Van in the mutton busting at the next rodeo?" Jimmy asked Trey.

"Of course, but I believe Marie will outride him. That girl dipped deeply into the Cahill gene pool. I believe she could ride a bull and declares she's going to have a buckle like Aunt Jodie's someday," Trey said.

"That sounds like Novaline. I'm hoping Rainey, here, is more feminine but I'm not holding my breath," Jimmy laughed. "Tell me, when you think of the lifestyle you had before all this, do you ever wish for anything different?"

"Not one time. How about you?" Trey asked.

Jimmy slowly shook his head. "Old George Carlin said that some folks get so tied up in making a living they forget to make a life. I feel like I need to drop down on my knees every single day and give thanks for those two days I had with this bunch in kindergarten, and that the good Lord let me remember them. It's the broken road that led me home to Jodie, as the song says."

"Something else George Carlin says," Rance said, "is that we are too guilty of multiplying our possessions and reducing our values. I'm glad Stella made me commit to a lifetime thing and wasn't willing to just be my fence-hopping mistress. We wouldn't have these three kids and another on the way if I'd had what I wanted in the beginning."

"How about you, Jack? You ever look back?"

"Not one time. I'm just grateful Dee came home to me. I missed her like the devil those years she was gone and feel like God has given both of us a second chance these past eight years. I wouldn't change a minute of it, not even when we argue, which is often and loud." He stopped long enough to pop the pacifier back into a dark-haired little baby girl's mouth.

"You don't have to ask me," Kyle said. "Greta and I were at cross horns from day one, and I wouldn't take any of it back. I'd be scared to." He chuckled as three children gathered around his legs and peered out between the rails of the corral fence. "She'd sue me for child support."

Cathy rolled her wheelchair across the yard as fast as she could. "Hey, you two, make room for the auntie who needs a front row seat."

"Where's Kent?" Trey asked.

"Oh, he's parking the van. I just made him let me out so I wouldn't miss anything. Lorraine is right behind us. She's got Melinda with her," Cathy said. Married six years now to Kent and a part of the extended Cahill family, she and her husband and daughter, Melinda, lived in Ardmore and ran a small oil company.

A commotion in the middle of the corral took their attention. Jimmy and Jodie's son, Ratch, was lying on the ground, his glasses knocked off. A child twice his size stood over him, shaking his fist. Before a teacher or mother could get across the corral, Ratch was on his feet and had tackled the child. Novaline, his younger sister, took stock of the situation and came running. She flattened the little boy's nose and yelled as she knocked him to the ground, "Don't never ever hit my brother again."

Ratch sat on him and Novaline continued to slap the boy until he screamed for his mommy to come rescue him.

Jodie looked across at Jimmy who was laughing so hard that tears ran down his cheeks into the deep dimples she loved so much. How could he laugh when his son was in the middle of his very first fight? It wasn't funny.

Junior's mother came running from the sidelines. "Get those hoodlums off my son. Why did they hit him? He didn't do anything."

Rosy hung on to Marie's shirt collar to keep her out of the fray. "Girl, you stay right here. Ratch and Novaline can take care of themselves."

"And that goes for you, too, Emalee. Jodie will take care of it," Stella said.

"He hit my brother and called him four eyes and he knocked his glasses off." Novaline came out of the fighting mass telling everything in a four-year-old lisp.

Junior's mother grabbed him by the shirt collar. "You did what? I've told you not to make fun of other children. Do you want to sit on the hot bus while the other children are having a good time?"

Junior shook his head. "No, Momma."

"Then you apologize to this little boy, and don't you ever pick on a child who wears glasses again."

Junior glared at both Crowe children and apologized but Jodie had no doubt there would be more battles in the future.

"Everything all right?" Rosy asked when the fracas was over.

"For today. I think he's probably enough like his father that he'll live to fight again but hopefully he'll think twice before he picks on the Crowe kids again," Jodie said.

"Who is that kid anyway?" Jimmy wiped at his eyes.

"That would be Joel Curtis's son," Kyle answered.

Jimmy shook his head and laughed even harder.

"What's so funny? Trey asked.

"History doth repeat itself," he answered.